Perilously Pink

JOANN KEDER

Publisher: Purpleflower Press

ISBN: · 978-1-953270-07-8

First Edition July, 2022

Edited by: Michele E. Gwynn

Cover Design by: Molly Burton with Cozy Cover Designs

Also by Joann Keder

<u>Piney Falls Mysteries</u>

Welcome to Piney Falls

Saving Piper Moonlight

Tales of Naybor Manor

Lavender's Tangled Tree

<u>Charming Mysteries</u>

Oceanberry Blues

Tangerine Troubles

<u>Emory Bing Mysteries</u>

<u>The Case of the Half-Baked Bing</u>

<u>The Case of the Rootbeer Bungle</u>

<u>The Case of the Fudged Features</u>

<u>The Case of the Chunky, Funky Monkey</u>

<u>The Case of the Clairvoyant Carrot</u>

<u>The Case of the Vegan Vixen</u>

<u>The Case of the Cream Cheese Caper</u>

<u>Pepperville Stories</u>

The Story of Keilah

Secrets and Sunflowers

Franniebell and Purple Wonder

Be the first to hear about new releases! Sign up for my newsletter here:

http://www.joannkeder.com

Acknowledgments

Thank you as always to my street team. Without you, this product wouldn't reflect my vision. Each successful writer needs not just one but many people in their corner, helping at all stages of development. I'm especially fond of the team of people I've assembled; each an expert in their own way. That includes the talented and extremely helpful, Morgan Meister, always quick-with-a-name, Andy Gold, the jill-of-all-trades Barbara Carter and the Keder Readers. I'm fortunate that you are willing to share your personal areas of expertise with me. Doug, Mackensie, Barbara, Meghan, Elise, Sarah, Laura and many others who answer endless seemingly nonsensical questions–you are appreciated!

*It's not enough to have lived. We should be determined
to live for something."*
Winston S. Churchill

*For all of the hardworking young women in this world.
In particular: Meghan, Mackensie, Laura, Morgan,
Jayden, Bryanna and Lauren. Thank you for being
quick with a smile.*

Characters

Feather Jones—paranormal investigator and salon owner
Tug Muehler—her entrepreneur boyfriend
Gemini Reed–retiree and amateur detective
Leo Reed–Gemini's husband, recovering from illness
Howard Beachmont–Gemini's next-door neighbor
Olive Thomas–Tug's business partner and friend to Feather and Gemini
Stevie—new salon employee
Mr. Beasley—Gemini and Howard's neighbor
Jayden Ko—nicest person in paranormal group
Tag Muehler Junior—Tug's older brother
Rigg Muehler—Tug's nephew and Tag Junior's son
Chugg Muehler—Tug's uncle
Martine Muehler—Tag Junior's ex-wife and Rigg's mother
Diego Betz—murder victim

Feather Jones was running through a long tunnel. There was water dripping on her head and the smell was something familiar to her, a mixture of vanilla and cooked spinach.

Don't stop. Keep running. Get to the end.

Out of breath, she paused, placing her hands on her knees. She sensed a presence behind her, but she was so exhausted she couldn't run any further.

Like a black cloud, it seeped around her body and began squeezing.

"I'll do what you ask!" She begged. "Just tell me what it is and this time, I'll do it."

In her dream state, she knew as soon as it loosened its grasp, she would run again. She could get away this time.

You must listen carefully, Feather Jones. You've been trying to escape me, but you can't outrun fate. The people you care about are in danger.

She attempted to nod, though her head was locked in tight, so she blinked her acceptance.

Turmoil threatens to explode the portal
The house of turns is a façade
Find the sheep made of steel, it will save you

The entity eased its grip. She tried running but her legs were wobbly, unsteady appendages that wouldn't move. She could see the bright sunlight ahead of her, a symbol of safety and comfort.

A lone hooded figure walked toward her at a leisurely pace.

"Help!" she screamed. "Please get me out of here! I can't move!"

The figure loped along until it was just out of reach. She strained to view the face.

"Help me! Please! I'm almost out of time!"

The figure turned and removed its hood. She recognized one broken tooth. "Tug! Please help me! Don't leave me here!"

"Babe! You're covered in sweat and your screams most likely woke the neighbors. Did you have that dream again?"

"Did you knock four times?" An unattached body called from behind the thick, wooden door.

"Yes. Is there something else I need to do?" Feather stood in front of, or rather behind the *Fold-Em and Go* laundromat, waiting for the okay to enter a hidden room. She wasn't much for secret societies, or for clubs, but an ominous note left in front of her apartment made it sound like she couldn't operate a paranormal investigation agency in Charming without belonging.

The door squeaked dramatically as it opened, revealing a tall, chestnut-haired woman with impeccable makeup. She was adorned in a pink cape. Most surprising was the gem-encrusted ruby red catsuit covering her body.

"And you are?"

"Feather...Jones. I thought that was obvious." Now

she was certain this was a mistake. "Maybe I should come back another time. You seem busy." She glanced beyond the woman, where something steamed in a large pot. It was just like the late-night horror movies she used to watch, where the unsuspecting guest of honor was thrown into the stew at the end.

"I was just pulling your leg." She stood aside and opened the door wide. "Of course, I know who you are. Come on in, Feather! We've been expecting you."

She moved aside so Feather could view the eclectic mix of people and décor.

A sound system boomed with rapid drumbeats that some of the guests were nodding and dancing to. When Feather ventured into the room, the music stopped, and the dancers and boppers stared at the interloper.

This was exactly the reason she avoided large crowds. A combat boot-wearing, pink-haired stylist with attitude wasn't a common sight in little seaside Charming, Oregon.

Clutching the mysterious invitation in her hand, she proceeded on the balls of her feet, serving both to make her look taller as well as to walk quieter. Neither seemed to matter to these strange faces.

She observed a room of motionless beings, people of all shapes and sizes, some covered in elaborate makeup and others wearing feathery masks. They all had two things in common; they were wearing the same pink capes, and most disturbing, they were all staring at her.

There was sweat running down the back of her neck, even though it was only forty-four degrees and she'd forgotten to turn on the heat in her car. Her heart was beating so fast and hard it felt like it might leap out of her chest and race her for the door. Worst of all was the suffocating scent of sweaty bodies mixed with cinnamon and vanilla.

The connection between the vanilla in her dream and the crowd around her was not lost on Feather. It could be interpreted as a mix of vanilla and spinach, she thought. If so, it didn't bode well for what came next.

"This was a mistake. I don't belong here." She turned abruptly, bumping into the chest of the woman who let her in.

"We're all outcasts here. You're among friends."

Feather glanced at the white name tag she was wearing, "P.I.N.K. Vice President, Jayden K."

"Would you like some punch before we begin?"

Feather looked at the steaming pot again. Dry ice.

"Sure. I guess."

Her boyfriend and paranormal investigations business partner, Tug Muehler, warned her before she left to avoid suspicious drinks or food in case there was funny business.

"You never know who might want you dead, Feather."

"You're being a little dramatic, Tug. It's a party for people who speak to the dead, like me. I can't imagine their business is so slow they need another other-worldly client."

Jayden handed her a smoking cup and invited her to join the others.

Feather took a tiny sip of the strangely bitter liquid, half-hoping that if she was being poisoned that Tug would come looking for her, despite her protestations.

"I was curious when you called what P.I.N.K. stood for?"

"Paranormal Investigators of the Northwest," a short, round woman with blue glasses replied as she pushed by to get more punch.

"What is the "k" for?"

Jayden took a deep breath. "We've had some missteps as an organization. Phoebe over there," she pointed across the room to a tall, thin woman, whose makeup portrayed a white tiger and whose braids swirled around the top of her head, "told a family she'd banished their ghost. That's a level L skill and she only wishes she was there."

"What happened with the ghost? And what is level L?"

"Level L is a skill you have to prove you've mastered before you can put it on your business card or claim it to clients. Everyone here has a specialty. You see the man with the black and white mask?" Jayden pointed across the room, where a man stood, dressed half in white and half in black. His mask matched his outfit.

He reminded Feather of the old movies she and

Tug watched. His slicked back hair and stylish demeanor was perfect for the time.

"He's up to level M. His latest skill is seeing apparitions in 3-D."

She didn't realize she had to have permission to see them. If they weren't visible, they were rattling around in her head. "And what about the ghost that Phoebe handled?"

Jayden took a sip of her drink. For the first time, Feather noticed her elaborately polished nails, each one a different color and design.

"He was more of a demon, I think. Tortured the poor family until they left the house. They sued our national organization, who, in turn, paid them handsomely but busted us back to a lower rank. We used to be Gorillas and now we're back to kittens."

Feather suppressed a giggle. "You investigate ghosts as kittens?" So far, she hadn't seen anything leading her to believe these people were worthy of her time. She had a hair salon to run, and her side gig, ridding homes of spiritual presence, was more of a hobby. Tug's new protein bar business was where they needed to focus all of their energy.

Jayden touched her thick hair, which Feather could now plainly see was a wig. "You'll be surprised at the level of talent here. Kitten or not, we've done a lot of good in this town."

Feather looked down at the stiff paper in her hand, remembering what brought her here. "Your invitation, or rather, your demand made it seem dire. *You must attend our meeting, or we'll make sure you never work in this town again.'* I don't like to be threatened. I'm not hurting anyone by investigating paranormal activity. I've even helped a few––"

Jayden pressed a long finger to her lips and pointed to a dark, purple curtain at the back of the room.

With a murmur that swelled to an overwhelmingly powerful sound, everyone in the room began snapping their fingers.

"What's going on?" Feather whispered, half-afraid and half-fascinated.

"Our grand leader, whom we call Capu, is a hermit who rarely shows his face. When he started, he was the only "out" paranormal investigator on the coast. He paved the way for the rest of us."

"Why is he here today?"

This time it was Jayden who giggled. "To see you, silly. You're going to help us regain our status as the best investigative group in the entire northwest. We'll go beyond Gorilla. We're going to become Pufferfish."

The curtain rustled and a hushed excitement spread over the room. A very small person wearing the same style of cape as the rest of the group appeared. Unlike the rest of the P.I.N.K. members, this person covered their face with a long hood.

The person made their way to the center of the room, accompanied by the finger snaps of the group. When they reached the center, the snapping stopped, and the room was so still that Feather could hear the sound of her own breath.

"You're supposed to put positive energy into the room," Jayden whispered.

Unsure of what exactly that meant, Feather closed her eyes and pretended she was concentrating. In reality, she was thinking of the best way to leave. Maybe there was a window in the bathroom. She could fake a headache. Her employees in the salon were masterful at that art. Especially on the days difficult clients were scheduled.

She felt a tap on her shoulder and opened her eyes. The mysterious Capu stood before her.

"Remove my hood and look away," a low voice commanded.

Suppressing every negative feeling she had about this situation, Feather did as she was told. Tug was going to have a field day with this when she told him. *"You should have stayed home and watched Bachelor Bakeries with me. I told you it was a mistake."*

Everyone turned battery-powered candles on, where they'd come from, she had no idea. They pointed them at Capu.

"You can look at me now, child."

She turned her head and braced herself for whatever—whoever—was underneath that hood. The nightmares she'd been experiencing lately ended in a similar manner. "This better not be a warped version of my boyfriend," she muttered under her breath.

Steeling herself, she opened her eyes, ready to take on whatever might be in front of her. The person who stood before her had never entered her dreams before. Not even once.

"Are you kidding me?"

Voices in the room gasped at Feather's reaction.

"How are you involved in this?"

Chapter Two

GEMINI

"Did I tell you that my new neighbor at Charming Retirement Village is a silver fox?" Olive Thomas, Gemini's fellow retiree, pretended to fan her face. "He's a former body builder. Reminds me of Feather's Tug, if he were a few decades younger."

Gemini Reed nodded and smiled. It wasn't like her to be so disinterested in Olive's stories. She'd grown rather fond of them, to her surprise. Today, however, she wanted to go home and curl up in a ball. She glanced up at the clock, dismayed to find it was only ten-thirty. She'd committed to staying in the Friendship Room until noon.

Gemini convinced Feather to turn the break room of *Feather Works Hair Salon* into a coffee and conversation corner, where people could come and talk about whatever they wanted before their appointments. It was a way to relieve the beautician's stress as well as the client's.

"What else is new, Olive? What about your power bar business with Tug?"

"Oh, heavens, girl. It's going better than we ever hoped. I recruited a few gals from my retirement apartments to help. They come over on Tuesday and Thursday mornings and get everything baked. We do three flavors of Tug Bars a week. I do all of the icing myself in the afternoons, and then Tug comes to help me bag them on Fridays. We're gonna need factory space soon!" Olive clapped her hands together and rocked in her seat.

Gemini definitely felt ill. Now that she'd had her tea and a peppermint, her normally strong stomach was complaining.

"I'm so happy for you, Olive." Her head felt heavy. She always told her daughter Sophia to hold still when that happened and let it pass.

"Gemini Reed, your face is positively green. Grapevine Green, the color you told me to paint my kitchen." When Gemini didn't laugh, Olive stood and placed her hand on Gemini's forehead. "Feverish. I'm gonna say one-hundred and one. My ride's going to be here soon. I'll have him drop you at home on his way. He's forever telling me his job isn't to be my personal taxi, but just this once, he won't mind."

Olive placed her arm underneath Gemini's elbow, urging her to stand.

"You don't have to..." She looked up at Olive and smiled weakly. "Yes. That sounds good. Feather won't be in today. Will you ask Stevie-the-new-girl, to clean up and turn off the lights? She can take the rest of the lemon bars home with her. I know her brother lives with her, and he is a healthy eater."

As she attempted to stand, her knees turned to spaghetti and gave out from underneath her. She tumbled to the ground, hitting her head on the chair seat on the way down.

Though her eyes were closed, she could hear Leo, her beloved husband of over thirty years, telling her everything would be all right. His smile wasn't a vision, but a feeling of warmth.

You're in good hands, love.

"Don't leave me, Leo," she tried to whisper, but her mouth wouldn't form the words.

When she opened her eyes again, she heard machines beeping. Gemini tried putting her hand to her head, where a mysterious pain emanated, but found they were both tied down.

"Mrs. Reed? Glad to see you're awake," a voice, far too perky for Gemini's liking, remarked. "How are you feeling? We had to tie your hands down. You kept trying to pull the dressing off your head wound."

As she was coming to, she realized her head wasn't her only source of pain. Her abdomen was equally upset. "What happened?"

As her vision returned, a nurse came into view and removed her arm restraints. "Your appendix ruptured. When you stood to leave the salon, you passed out."

It was coming back to her now. "What about Olive? She was holding on to me. Is she okay?"

"Two stitches, but she's fine. You, on the other hand, received a sprain to your left arm and twenty stitches to your scalp, in addition to the loss of your appendix. No excitement for you for the foreseeable future." The nurse patted her good arm comfortingly. "On the bright side, there is an entire waiting room full of people who wanted to make sure you were okay. You must be a very popular woman."

As much as it warmed her heart to think of all of her friends waiting for news of her condition, she couldn't muster any excitement for guests. "Can you tell them thank you? And to please come back tomorrow?"

The nurse chuckled and shook her head. "Only one visitor at a time. You're here for rest, not social hour. Your daughter arrived about thirty minutes ago and has been pacing the halls. Would you like me to get her?"

She was not in any frame of mind to see Sophia either, but her uptight daughter wouldn't be kind to the staff if they made her wait too long.

"Yes, tell her to come in." Gemini closed her eyes, hoping for a few more minutes to prepare for whatever accompanied Hurricane Sophia.

"Mother! I was so worried!"

She rushed to Gemini's side and put her head on her mother's chest. "We could have lost you, Mother. I've been a wreck!"

Gemini stroked her daughter's wavy hair with her

I.V. arm and winced when she tried to bend it. "I'm going to live. Or so I've been told."

"You're coming to live with us. Brandon has already begun preparing the guest house. We can build another space for Taurus's second toy room. I'll hire 'round-the-clock care for you, and—"

"Wait, please!" Her head throbbed, reminding her that whispering was all her body was capable of right now. "Let's see what the doctor says first. I have many friends here who will happily care for me. I'd hate for my grandson to lose his second playroom."

"We're not arguing over that today, Mother. But soon. If you refuse to come stay with me, I'll take steps to have you cared for around the clock in your home. Would that suit you better?"

It wasn't like Sophia to give in so easily. Her husband, Brandon, must've been upset by the potential disruption to their lives.

"That would be much nicer, yes."

"I'll begin interviewing for help immediately. Does it hurt, Mother? Will you need pain pills? I've got many in my purse."

"No, daughter. I'm fine. It's going to set me back is all. I have plans, you see, for a new business."

Sophia gently pushed Gemini's hair off her forehead. "Oh, Mother. You're hallucinating. We're in the hospital and you've had an accident."

The day before, she and Feather were discussing Gemini's amateur detective skills when Feather encouraged her to open a business.

"You can use the Friendship Room space, Gem. It would be so cool to have a detective agency here!"

"People come to me, looking for solutions. I might as well turn it into a proper business. What about the original intent of the Friendship Room, Feather? I don't want to turn anyone away who just wants a listening ear."

"Don't worry, Gemini. Tug will put up a partition or something. We'll figure it out."

Sophia would tell her how dumb it was until she actually saw her mother in action.

"Never mind. You're right. I must've made the whole thing up. I'd like to get more rest now."

She drifted off, hoping to feel her husband's warmth once again.

Feather blinked repeatedly. Being a paranormal investigator, she spent a lot of time viewing apparitions, questioning whether they were real. "Mr. Beasley, you're Gemini's neighbor, right?"

He nodded and rubbed the velvet collar of his dark pink robe. "That's my street name. Here, where we're all free to be ourselves, you may call me Capu."

It was hard to reconcile the tiny, frail man, who spent his days in a lawn chair waving at traffic, with the seemingly powerful head of the P.I.N.K. organization.

"I have so many...," Her phone buzzed.

"Give it to me," Jayden held out a slender hand with one long, onyx-colored nail. "The rules are that phones are on silent. You don't get any warnings. First time offense means I take it until the end of the evening. Second offense means you'll pay me a hefty sum if you want it returned."

Feather attempted to take a quick glance at the

screen before handing it over, but the screen went dark. "What if my boyfriend is in trouble? He doesn't have any family he can call."

Tug's wealthy family cut him off when they realized he wasn't going into the family business, Muehler Enterprises. He never spoke of them.

"He'll call your friend Gemini."

She smiled knowingly as Feather opened her mouth to question how they knew any of her friends. "We do our research." Jayden stuck the phone in her bra. "If you follow me, we'll fill out the necessary forms. You can't actually attend a meeting until all of your paperwork is on file. It's an insurance thing."

"You follow Jayden," Mr. Beasley echoed. "She's been a member here almost as long as me. We'll have a nice chat later." He patted the top of her head, like she was a neighborhood child who lost their pet. "You must give me Gemini's recipe for orange drop cookies. She brought some over last week and they're divine."

He continued his procession through the room, with a rockstar-like presence. Attendees grabbed his cape and reached for his hands.

If she hadn't seen it with her own eyes, Feather wouldn't have believed it. The transformation from frail elderly man to commanding presence was something to behold. Gemini would find this so amusing.

"What if I don't want to become a member? Despite your threatening invitation, I thought this was a support group for other paranormal investigators. I'm only here to test the waters." Feather folded her arms and stood firmly in place. These oddballs weren't going to control her.

Jayden shook her head. "This is how it's going to be? We were under the impression you were easier to work with. Had we known otherwise, we would have interviewed the Pansy Pants Paranormal from Tellum. She's not as gifted as you, but she's been begging to join us for years."

Feather unfolded her arms and continued reading the bright fuchsia paper she carried with her. *"Miss Jones, we've been following your successes with Light as a Feather, Paranormal Investigations. Your presence, as stated above, is required, though we'd love for you to meet other paranormal investigators in the area. We're having an informal gathering for drinks and cookies on Saturday at 2 p.m. Our address is 55 and a half Pelican Lane. Knock four times on the door and wait to be ushered in."*

She shoved the paper in Jayden's face. "Does that sound like I'm being interviewed? I think I'd like to leave now."

"Please wait!" Jayden begged. "Come into my office and I'll explain everything. If you still want to leave after that, I won't stop you."

Feather looked around the octagon-shaped room, unsure of where an office could be hiding. More out of curiosity than actual drive, she agreed. "I'll give you ten minutes. I'm a busy woman and I'm sure Tug is worried. He wouldn't normally call so many times."

Jayden motioned for her to follow as she disappeared behind another of the seemingly endless beaded curtains. Next to the door with a sign overhead stating, *"We gotta go. Spirits don't,"* was another room with a pink door. Jayden unlocked it and let them inside.

She sat down at a glass desk and motioned for Feather to sit on the other side. Reaching into the cupboard beside her, she pulled out a folder marked *'Confidential'* and slid it across the table.

"Just the basics. Your name, address, how long you've been experiencing spirit connections. Oh, and what level of skill you have. We require a thirty dollar signup fee, cash or card. Paper products aren't cheap."

Feather opened the folder. "I have no idea what your levels are. I thought this was just a casual gathering. Well, casual but threatening. Your invitation was confusing, as we've already discussed."

Jayden shook her head and sighed. "Mortimer W. has been our acting secretary for too long. His gifts do not include writing."

"Is that the same Mortimer W. who writes weekly complaint letters to the editor of the paper? I had to quit reading them, they were feeding my anxiety."

"The very same." Jayden pulled out another folder. "I couldn't tell you about this in front of everyone else."

Feather opened the folder and pulled out four large black and white photos. "Is that our mayor?" She picked up the first photo and brought it close to her face. "It's so grainy, it's hard to tell."

"Yes, that's him. One of our members, Phyllis

Pembroke, received frequent calls to come to his home. It isn't mandatory to give us details about clients, only the actions you perform, but she bragged that she was the only one in our group who had spoken to the dead inside the mayor's mansion."

"So what's the problem?"

"Well, Lucy B., she's the nosy one in our group, started noticing that every time the mayor's wife was out of town at a conference, that's when Phyllis was called to get rid of the spirits."

Feather shook her head in disgust. "Now I get it. Someone with a telephoto lens took these shots. I can see now, it's the mayor and Lucy."

She briefly thumbed through the rest of the photos. "And that's really why you're busted back to kitten rank?"

"Partly. I told you about Phoebe's mix up. She tried ridding a home of a spirit, only to find later it wasn't an ordinary spirit, but a demon. The owners of the home had to move to get away from it." Jayden wiped her eyes carefully with a tissue.

"Someone contacted the national organization and gave them all of this information, thus our kitten status. It makes us sound like a sorry bunch of ghost hunters, but I can assure you, there's a lot of talent here. Morale is low and we need some wins."

"That doesn't explain why you want me." Feather adjusted herself uncomfortably. "I'm nobody special."

"We've been watching you, Feather Jones. You're going places."

Feather blushed. "What do you mean? I haven't been doing this very long. I'm not even sure I'm doing it right." She studied Jayden's face, trying to find any trace of dishonesty.

"Your work on the Brigadoon Mansion —impressive!"

Last month, Feather spent hours in the basement of the mansion, trying to communicate with Sergeant Funk. Gemini researched the history of the home and discovered the good sergeant had been sitting in the basement when a tidal wave hit. Together, they'd convinced him to leave.

"It wasn't just me. My friend Gemini helped. And Tug, he's my boyfriend. I guess you already know that. He let me bounce ideas off him all night long for three weeks. We're a great team."

"It's *your* investigative skills we're interested in, for a couple of reasons. We want you to find out exactly who the spirit is that's been haunting the laundromat. Patrons of the *Fold 'Em and Go* have reported being shoved, kicked, and punched. Every single member has tried at one time or another to talk to him or her. Every time, it's the same message; *You're not the one. Bring her here.*"

"So it wasn't a choice between me and someone in Tellum. This is because you think I'm the one the spirit is referring to."

"It's all a guessing game, isn't it?" Jayden winked at Feather, displaying bedazzled eyelids. "In all seriousness, if the laundromat loses any more business, they'll

have to close and then we're out of a meeting place."
She looked around the room. "It suits us, it's quiet, and
no one bothers our group. We don't want to move."

Jayden placed her long fingers on either side of her
face. "The worst part is that the owner is so desperate
for help that he contacted the organization from the
next county over. The P.I.N.J. are already petitioning
to have us removed from the national charter. If they
are able to rid the *Fold 'Em and Go* of its spirit, that
will be the last straw for us."

"What does the 'j' stand for? Jackals?"

Jayden rolled her eyes. "They're jaguar level. Four
above us. It would be a true disgrace if someone from
that group solved this mystery."

She could feel her chest tightening, something that
happened with increasing frequency during her work-
day. "How did you really hear about me?"

Jayden reached in the drawer and pulled out a flyer
with *Light as a Feather Paranormal Investigations*
scrawled across the top. "Found this on the bulletin
board of the laundromat, right by the soap dispenser."

"Oh," Feather replied sheepishly. "If I had known I
was stepping on someone's toes, I never would have
hung one there."

"No matter. There is one other thing we'll require
of you though."

"I've heard about hazing in secret groups. If that's
the case, I'm out of here." Another of Tug's worries. If
he was right about all of this, there would be no living
with him.

"No, we don't have the time or energy for that. Your test will be a challenge we've never asked of a newbie before. We'd like you to work with another potential member, someone who hasn't yet demonstrated paranormal skills, but is enthusiastic about learning."

Feather leaned back in the chair. Recently, one of her stylists at *Feather Works Salon* quit to pursue a career in salmon fishing. Two more were on vacation. She barely had time to sleep. "I suppose with my whole team involved, we could manage to–"

"Oh, no!" Jayden lurched forward. "You can't tell anyone! All of our work is completely confidential. You haven't gotten to the bottom form in the folder, the confidentiality form."

There was no way. Her plate was entirely too full.

"My team is very discreet, I promise you. My life is too busy as it is and if we can't work together, I won't be able to accept your invitation."

"I believe you, I do. But it's much more complicated than you'd think. The person you're going to train came to us with a proposition. He would donate ten thousand dollars to our coffers in exchange for his training. There was one very large string attached... He insisted his mentor would be you."

"But...how could he... I'm not even officially a member."

Jayden shrugged her shiny red shoulders. "That's what I said. I even offered to train him myself. Between my job and this group, I barely have time to breathe. It didn't matter. He said no. He was adamant his instructor would be Feather Jones."

Feather opened her mouth to disagree. She was certain this whole experience would lead to bad things.

"I possess the gift of precognition, Feather. On cheesy commercials, they call themselves psychics. I know what's in your head, maybe before you do. I know about your nightmares. Maybe your coming here is fate. You help us, and I can help you with your sleeping situation."

Jayden took a deep breath and turned her chair so that it faced away from Feather. "If you don't agree, our potential member and his money will most likely find a place with P.I.N.J., another blow to a charter barely standing as it is. You can understand now why you received such a sternly worded invitation. Our hands are tied."

Feather's head swam as she thought of all the bullies from her high school years who might think it funny to force her to train them. There were more bad experiences than she could count. But to her knowledge, none of them had that kind of money to throw around.

"I don't understand who would do this. Who thinks I should train them? I can't think of anyone who would want my help. If it was a former client, they would have just told me..." The hairs on Feather's arms rose, a telltale sign that a spirit was nearby.

Jayden pursed her maroon lips. "The other newbie is your boyfriend Tug's brother."

Chapter Four

GEMINI

"Where am I?"

Gemini blinked, the harsh fluorescent light blasting her face. She was keenly aware of the searing pain in her abdomen. "Leo? Where are you?"

She felt a cool hand on hers. "Mother? Daddy is still in the care center recovering from his stroke, remember?"

"Now I remember," she whispered. "When can I go home?"

Sophia sighed. It was a familiar and oddly comforting sound.

"Mother, I'm not sure you're going home. You are getting up there in age, and as such I don't feel right letting you recover on your own. I tried getting you a room in the place Daddy lives, but–"

"That's for people who are really sick! I'm just temporarily sidelined." Protest, in any form, it seemed, caused her head to throb. "Ugh. Sophia, could we get some ice for my head?"

"Yes, of course."

Her daughter disappeared and returned quickly with a cool pack. She placed it gently on Gemini's head. "How's that?"

Gemini jumped when the ice touched her stitches, and Sophia moved it slightly.

"Better. Thanks, hon."

"As I was saying, I tried getting you space in the care center, but they are full right now. Brandon is currently interviewing nurses. The doctors say you can go home in two days, but we won't allow that unless we've got a caretaker in place."

She wanted to disagree, but in her current state, it didn't seem worth the effort.

"How is Taurus? Is his second playroom safe?"

Now that she was remembering their last conversation, she thought it ludicrous he had more than one room full of toys.

"Your grandson is just fine. He's begun toddler karate. His teacher says he's the smartest one in the class."

"That's nice."

"Oh, and mother, you've had several people trying to visit, but I left strict orders for you to be left in peace.

Gemini's eyes popped open. "Who?"

"Oh, that neighbor of yours, Howard something–"

"Beachmont."

"Yes, he brought flowers and I had them promptly thrown in the trash. We can't have a surprise allergy pop up. Then there was that goth girl at the beauty salon."

"Feather? She's not Goth."

"She's been here more than once. She and her muscle-y boyfriend. What an odd pair. Oh, and then the boyfriend came with a little old lady. Pecan or something..."

"Olive." Her voice was just above a whisper, even as she forced it to be louder.

"Yes, that's it. The goth girl's boyfriend and Olive came together. They brought candy, even though I strictly forbade it. Then the boyfriend came again. He's a persistent one."

Gemini felt herself drifting off. For once, she didn't feel a bit guilty about falling asleep while Sophia droned on and on.

The next time she awoke, the bag ice from her head was lying in a puddle of water on her chest and her headache was gone. She looked around the room, trying to remember what had taken place before her nap. She closed her eyes again, visions of Sophia's diatribe coming back to her. She heard someone clear their throat and she raised her head. "Sophia? I'm sorry I fell—"

To her surprise, Tug Muehler was sitting in a large chair, his leg bouncing.

He jumped to his feet when he saw her eyes open. "Gem? We've all been so worried!"

"How did you get in? I thought Sophia set up a moat around this castle complete with armed guards."

It felt good to joke and to see a friend.

"Your daughter went home for the evening. She's coming back tomorrow. The head nurse for this floor bought some of our Tug Bars for her kids and loved them. I told her I'd give her a big discount if she'd let me in."

"It doesn't hurt that you're easy on the eyes." Gemini winked, then winced as it pulled a stitch.

"I suppose not. It can be helpful," he replied without a bit of conceit. "How are you feeling?"

"I think I'll live. Sophia says I can go home in two days, but she and Brandon are hiring someone to care for me, so I won't have free reign for the foreseeable future."

"That's why I wanted to talk to you now."

"Sophia mentioned you'd been here several times. Thank you for bringing flowers. I'm sorry my daughter confiscated them." She attempted to push herself to the seated position but the pain in her abdomen prevented her from getting that far.

"Let me help." Tug placed one forearm under each of her armpits and lifted her until she was exactly where she wanted to be. He poured her a cup of water and handed it to her.

"You're nice to have around." She took a sip and gave the cup back to him. "Tell me what it is that you wanted to talk about?"

"Where am I? What's going on?" A voice from the

other side of a curtained divide interrupted their conversation.

"You're in the hospital, Dorothy. You broke your hip, remember? Your son will be here at four," a disembodied voice replied.

"Oh, all right then."

A woman poked her head around the curtain. "Sorry, my aunt has memory issues. We go through this about every hour."

"The poor dear," Gemini clucked in sympathy. "At least I still have my faculties. Don't I, Tug? I want to make sure."

"You're perfect, Gem." Tug squeezed her hand.

"All right then. Let's get to it. What did you want to talk to me about?"

"Two things, actually. First, Feather went to a meeting for the paranormal society and came home extremely upset. I'd been trying to get a hold of her about your accident, so when I told her, of course that took precedence. We haven't talked about it since."

"My sweet girl. What do you think is bothering her? Are they cliquey? That's always a problem in small towns."

"She wouldn't say a word. We never keep things from each other, so it's really bothering me."

"I'll see what I can do. I'll have privacy when I get home." She motioned over her shoulder toward the woman behind the curtain. "What else is bothering you?"

Tug sat on the edge of her bed. "Do you remember me telling you about my family?"

"Yes, I do. Your wealthy parents never believed in you and when you refused to go into the family business, they disowned you."

"That's correct. Well, mostly."

A nurse walked in and stared uneasily at Tug.

"He's my nephew," Gemini said quickly. "He surprised me and came up from Piney Falls. Wasn't that wonderful?"

The nurse's expression eased. "Oh, how nice! I'll let you two visit. I'll be bringing your dinner in ten minutes, Mrs. Reed. Would you like an extra tray for your nephew?"

"Oh, no. I'm eating with Feather." Tug paused when he realized what he'd said. "I mean, I'm eating with my brother. Words get confused sometimes." He thunked his head playfully.

"For all of us," Gemini added.

When the nurse was gone, Gemini and Tug giggled together.

"That was close," she said. "Now finish telling me about your family!"

"Because I didn't go into the family business, they not only cut me out of my inheritance, but also stopped talking to me. Everyone except my grandma. Grandma Mitzi says I'm still in her will, but for now, I'm on my own."

"I do remember, dear. It was courageous of you to think with your soul and not your checkbook."

Tug nodded and continued. "Last week, my dad left a strange message on my phone. He hasn't done that in over two years."

"Is someone in your family ill?"

"It's my brother's kid. Dad's message said he wants me to contact Rigg and see if he'll talk to me."

"I didn't know you had any nieces or nephews!"

"They don't communicate with me either. According to Dad, Rigg—that's Tag Junior's son--has been acting strangely. He refused to speak for almost a year and is always in a bad mood. They sent him away to a special school to help straighten him out, thinking that would be the end of it. That's how my family thinks, throw money at the problem and it will go away."

Tug squeezed his eyes shut tightly, rubbing the bridge of his nose.

"Do you have any idea why your father would have contacted you specifically?"

"Oh, I'm positive I know why. Rigg is an outcast. Whatever his issues are, they can't understand him, just like me. Dad figured the older oddball could explain the younger."

In addition to her own aches and pains, Gemini felt a deep sadness for her friend. "I'm so sorry. It must be serious for your father to call you after all this time. Did he say what he wants?"

"The school Rigg attended was the Smiley Academy in Fassetville. I looked it up and discovered you were on the board until last year."

Gemini gasped. "That isn't a place you send a troubled child. It's a very specialized school for extremely bright children. They recognize each student's strengths and create individual educational plans. My Sophia excelled there. And you said, 'was.' He isn't anymore?"

"I read that on their website. In Dad's message, he mentioned Rigg getting kicked out of school so I should talk to him. I had lots of questions, so I called my Dad back and he didn't answer. This morning I got a call from his secretary. She said his contacting me was a mistake and I shouldn't bother him again. My family is notorious for keeping secrets."

As much as she was enjoying his visit, her energy was plummeting. "You'd like me to contact the school? You know that I quit the board when we moved to Charming, but I still have contacts there."

"Gem, I'd be so grateful. I need to understand what's going on with that kid. I don't trust anyone in my family to look out for him. The fact that my dad was so desperate that he called me means something suspicious is going on."

Chapter Five

FEATHER

Feather paused before opening the door to her apartment. She and Tug were in a good place. They never fought and rarely kept secrets. It was the relationship she'd dreamt of her entire adult life.

Knowing Tug's brother, Tag Muehler Junior, joined the P.I.N.K. organization just to spy on her was hard enough. Keeping it from the man she loved, nearly impossible.

She turned the doorknob, concentrating on displaying a natural smile and pleasant face. The rich smell of baked oatmeal filled her nostrils as Tug appeared, clad in a green *Feather Works Salon* apron.

"How'd it go? Did the kids play nice? It's your second time and I haven't heard anything yet. I'm starting to wonder if you're keeping something from me." He kissed her on the cheek and put a small piece of his latest project in her mouth. "Olive You Got. It's our newest Tug Bar creation."

"It's amazing, Tug." She held her hand under her mouth, catching the crumbs before they hit their freshly vacuumed carpet. "We were a little distracted after the first meeting. Gemini went to the hospital, remember?"

It embarrassed her that Gemini's hardship provided such a perfect out for her. Tug forgot to ask her about the first meeting, so she avoided the conversation, at least initially.

He took her hand and guided her to the couch. "I want to hear everything. Were they all wearing matching outfits? Do they have a secret language?"

She giggled. "You've been watching too many young adult streaming shows. Neither of those things happened. There was a very nice lady named Jayden. She thinks I'm talented–"

"Why wouldn't she?"

Feather gulped. She'd already shared more than she should have. "She'd like me to join. I wasn't sure it was the right place for me, but there was a spirit in the room while we were talking. I heard the voice loud and clear. It told me this was where I needed to be." Shifting her weight in a mock show of discomfort gave Feather a reason not to look him in the eyes.

"You can't keep things from me, Feath. You might as well not even try."

Tug squeezed her hand and she squeezed back.

"No, I can't. That's what makes this–"

"It's those dreams you've been having. You're worried it has something to do with this new group."

You help us and I'll help you with your dreams.

When she declined to reply, he rubbed her arm. "Feath, what is it? I can tell you're still keeping something from me. We made a pact, remember?"

"No secrets in the Juehler Family." They'd joked that combining their names would result in something strange and used it only when speaking of their little family.

"Those dreams haunt me, whether my eyes are closed or open. I know there is a spirit trying to send me a message. I think about it all the time."

"We've never sat down and really discussed the riddle. What was the first one?"

"Turmoil threatens to explode the portal."

"Yeah. That sounds pretty messy," Tug teased. "What could that mean?"

"A portal can be a place or a person."

"I bet it's your salon. It's been a stressful place lately with everyone always at each other's throats. Have you thought any more about bringing in a therapist?"

Feather laid her head on Tug's chest. "Even the mention of help upsets them. Stevie-the-new-girl looks like a scared little rabbit every time they go at it. Poor thing. I bet she'll be out the door soon."

He stroked her hair and kissed the top of her head.

"Number two. The house of turns is a façade. That one is really confusing. A merry-go-round? What else turns?"

"Your stomach when I make greens shakes?"

She reached back and slapped his stomach playfully. "I doubt there is a spirit brave enough to warn me about that."

"What's number three?"

"Find the sheep made of steel. It could be anything —even a hair dryer at the salon."

"Like finding a needle in a haystack," he remarked.

"All of this is unsettling, Tug." She flipped around and put her chin in the middle of his chest. "I'm afraid if I don't solve these riddles, harm will come to you and Gemini. You two are the most important people in my life."

Tug raised his head off the couch and looked at her earnestly. "You don't have to worry about me, babe. And you don't have to worry about the extra time commitment to your new group. I promised to support you and that's exactly what I'll do. I want you to do it. Make them see how talented you are."

She changed the subject quickly. "Tell me about Gem. What's the latest? Is she going to be released soon?"

"Tomorrow," Olive announced from the kitchen, startling them both. "Her daughter hired a nurse. She should be in the care center with her husband, if you ask me."

"Thanks, Olive," Feather replied. "I should see if there's anything I can do. She's always doing things for us."

"Oh, no. Her daughter gave strict instructions. She's not allowed visitors or outings. Poor thing. She'll be in prison," Olive continued. "I hate to be a busybody, but I'm gonna check on this nurse and make sure she's a good egg. You know how Gemini has bad luck with nurses."

Gemini's husband, Leo, was the victim of an unscrupulous nurse and her boyfriend.

It occurred to her that Olive wasn't usually cooking in their kitchen. "Wait, why are you here baking when you have that nice kitchen space at the retirement home?" Feather looked at Tug. "I thought you guys had it all worked out?"

"We did," Olive replied. "But I got to visiting with the new resident hunk, Donald. He batted those baby greens at me, and I was mush for an hour. The bars needed to come out in forty-five, so you can understand what happened."

"They had to call the fire department," Tug whispered. "Olive is banned from the communal kitchen for good."

"Glad you're okay, Olive," Feather called.

"You've looked so tired lately. Don't want you giving someone a mohawk if they ask for a light trim," Olive commented before returning to the kitchen.

Tug's face twisted. "I hate to see you like this, Feath. That counselor you wanted to bring into the salon, I think you should talk to her about your dreams. She might have a different perspective."

Olive reappeared, now wearing her *Seventy and Sexy* apron, flour covering her cheeks. "You wanna try this batch, Tug? You thought I used too much orange oil in the last one."

"This seems like a lot of work for one person. Even a machine like you, Olive. What happened to the two part-timers you told me about?" Feather asked.

"A little fire and those two are embarrassed to be seen with me," Olive sniffed. "No work ethic at all."

"Olive and I will work out of our kitchen for now. Maybe once Gemini feels better we can use her kitchen too." Tug patted Feather's leg as a signal to let him up.

Feather looked up at the clock. Four-thirty. "I think I'll try a nap right now, if you two don't mind."

She kissed Tug and waved to Olive before finding the comfort of her dark bedroom. Though she struggled often with insomnia, Feather slipped into a deep sleep almost immediately.

Today she was running in a field full of flowers. They were beautiful, but tall and hard to navigate. The same dark spirit was following her, and she had to get away.

Three puzzles, Feather Jones. These are a matter of life and death.

She stopped running, feeling a sudden burst of self-confidence. "Exactly who are you?"

Turning around, she saw the entity encased in a pink robe. The hood fell back and this time it wasn't Tug. This time, she saw...herself.

Chapter Six

GEMINI

"This is overkill, Sophia. I'm perfectly fine walking into my own home."

When they pulled her out of the ambulance, she peeked through her hands. To her dismay, there were six neighbors standing in their yards ogling her.

Gemini covered her face as the Charming City Ambulance crew lowered the stretcher and wheeled her inside. Everyone within a four-block area would be out watching. "Small town folks live for flashing lights and sirens," she grumbled.

"Howdy, Gemini!" Mr. Beasley called from the comfort of his lawn chair, across the street. "Glad you're home now. Don't be a stranger!"

She waved but didn't look up. Of course he was watching

"Nonsense, Mother. I need to know you're well cared for." Sophia held the door open as they bumped the stretcher up the steps. "Careful, my mother is very fragile. If you break anything that isn't already broken, you'll be hearing from my husband's law firm," she warned.

"It's all right. I'm not that breakable." Gemini tried catching the gaze of one of the EMTs, hoping for a show of support, but the woman looked away. Sophia had already convinced the hospital to keep her on their extended stay floor for an extra week. She shuddered thinking of the cost.

When they had her settled in her bedroom, Gemini pushed pillows behind her back, trying to reach a sitting position.

"What do you think you're doing?" Sophia snapped.

"I'm going to do some reading. I need to calm my nerves after that embarrassing display for the neighbors." She reached over to her nightstand, where the novel she was reading before her hospitalization still sat. She winced as she stretched and immediately faked a cough so Sophia wouldn't suspect she was in pain from an activity.

"Could you get me some water, dear? And maybe a nice cup of tea? There's some chamomile in the kitchen."

She watched her daughter walk out and quickly scrolled through her phone, finding the number for Smiley Academy. A call to check on Tug's nephew wouldn't tax her. There was a brisk knock at the front door, and she set her phone down.

"If that's Howard, show him in," she called.

When there was no answer, she returned to her phone.

"Oh, that's a bug-a-boo of mine. Phones are for healthy communication only. You're not healthy yet, Mrs. Reed."

Gemini looked up, already irritated. She smelled the strong scent of antiseptic before she noticed a disagreeable woman standing in her doorway. Every angle on her body was pointed—her chin, elbows and shoulders. This woman was severe in every part of her being.

"I take it you're the nurse Sophia hired?"

"Skye Baker." She placed her hand in Gemini's and shook so firmly Gemini worried her good arm might come out of the socket. The woman's straight, dark hair flapped against her face as she pulled Leo's favorite rocking chair from the corner over to the side of the bed.

"Your daughter is concerned you'll try to do too much too soon. That's another bug-a-boo of mine; patients who think they are infallible. I'm here to tell you, you're not."

The lightness she'd felt in her chest being home again was now a heavy helpless lump.

"Oh, I see you're getting to know each other." Sophia set Gemini's tea on her nightstand and placed her hands on her hips. "She's the best, Mother."

"I am." Skye smiled with satisfaction. "I should have asked to see what you were giving my patient before you brought it in. I keep track of everything coming in and..." she pointed to Gemini's rear end with her pen.

Gemini shuddered. "I'm well past that stage of recovery, thank you."

"Not until you're able to walk around the block without assistance. We're going to start with your phone. I'll need that to be in my possession until this evening. I allow my patients thirty minutes of family conversation." She held out her hand expectantly.

Gemini frowned at Sophia. "No, that's not how this will work. I need to have my phone in case there is a problem with my husband or my grandson."

She crossed her hands over her chest. "Sophia, tell her," Gemini insisted.

"I'm going to have to agree with my mother on this, Ms. Baker. She needs access to her phone. There's rarely a day that goes by without a crisis of some kind."

Gemini's blood was boiling. This was turning into more of a hostage situation than a recovery. "I have plenty of good friends who will be happy to check on me. I don't need a prison guard."

"It's not how I like to work..." Skye shook her head. "All right. But if I see you spending rest-time on your phone, I'll have to confiscate it."

"May I speak with my daughter alone?"

"Of course. I'll wait in the hall. After that, I want to go over your fiber intake." Her shoes clacked against the wood floor as she left. Gemini envisioned her shoes being as pointy as the rest of her.

After Skye stepped out and closed the door,

Gemini folded her good arm over her chest. "Sophia, what were you thinking? That woman is horrible!"

"She's not what I was expecting either, but Brandon assured me her credentials are impeccable. He interviewed twenty different nurses, Mother," she said emphatically.

Now it was all making sense. Brandon's dislike for Gemini was behind this awful situation. He was sitting in his office right now, chuckling as he thought of Gemini locked away in her bedroom while Nurse Nightmare examined her stools.

"I'm going to find my own nurse. Someone who has a better understanding of my needs."

Sophia shook her head emphatically. "We've contracted her for this week and next. After that, you can find your own person. Can we agree upon that?"

Her daughter had three different tones; Mother, I'm irritated, Mother, I'm *extremely* irritated, and Mother I'm not backing down. This was the third option and there wasn't any point in arguing.

"I've got to get home. Taurus is helping his new nanny make supper tonight. Did I tell you he was taking classes at the Tater Tot Academy? Last week they made banana pudding."

"You did mention that. I can't wait for him to cook something wonderful for me."

Gemini suppressed a chuckle, thinking about the amount of energy that would require on her part. She didn't have enough for a kitchen cleanup of that magnitude today.

Sophia bent down and kissed her on either cheek. "I'll check in with you frequently. Meanwhile, please give Skye a chance! Aren't you always telling me to look underneath the surface? She may be the best nurse you've ever met."

"Yes, I'll do that," she answered, unconvinced. "Oh, Sophia, could you ask Skye to wait a few minutes before we talk about my fiber? I want to call and check on your father first."

"Okay. Love you, Mother."

"Love you too, dear."

The door closed and Gemini picked up her phone. Leo was doing the same, able to nod when he understood and eat small bites. She longed to touch his handsome face, but that would come soon enough. "Put the phone up to his ear, please. Yes, I'll wait."

Her pulse quickened just as it had while they were dating, when she used to call him for no reason at all. "Leo? It's me, sweetheart. I miss you so much. I'm a bit under the weather, so I won't be in for a few days. I'll make sure our favorite nurse, Trent, looks in on you. He'll be giving me updates. Oh, and Leo? Farrah doesn't make it out of the cave alive. I read ahead, sorry. I love you!"

She blew kisses into the phone, refusing to allow herself to feel sad. Her time was limited, and she needed to make one more call.

"Hello? Mariella? How are things going at Smiley Academy? This is Gemini Reed. Yes, we're doing just fine. We've decided to move to Charming permanently."

There was no use telling them about Leo's condition. That was for a different conversation.

"I wanted to ask you about a student. He's the grandson of a new friend and there were concerns about his care. His name is Rigg Muehler."

She heard a rustling at the door and put her hand over the phone. "Skye, I'm still speaking with my husband. Why don't you help yourself to a cup of tea? I'll be finished soon."

"Okay, Mrs. Reed. I'll caution you not to tire yourself. One of my bug-a-boos is a patient wearing themselves—"

"Thank you, Skye. I'll let you know when I'm done."

She waited until she heard the click of Skye's heels walking in the opposite direction.

"I'm sorry, Mariella. Finish what you were saying."

When the conversation ended, she dialed Tug's number.

"You were right. Your nephew wasn't there because of the gifted program. He was stored away. He had difficulties with the other kids, so they put him in classes for kids a year younger. The other interesting—"

The door flew open, banging against the coatrack Leo carved out of their first maple tree. "Aha! I didn't think you were talking to your husband. I'll be taking your phone, Mrs. Reed."

Feather Jones lived with one foot in two different worlds. In the paranormal world, there was a rhythm to their communication that she understood. Sometimes it came through in fragments, or in riddles as they had in her dreams. She was always able to understand, eventually, what was said.

Last night, as she waited for Tug to come to bed, someone named Morgan told her they'd watch over her today. It was comforting, even if she didn't quite understand why.

In the living beings' world, things weren't as clear cut. The constant bickering between her employees was filled with loaded words and late-night secret texts. She didn't understand how to fix it or how to help them. Sometimes she had clients who didn't communicate their wishes and she was left trying to make them happy with impossible expectations. Spirits were so much easier.

She glanced in her rearview mirror, checking for cars behind her with curious occupants. There were none. "You're being paranoid, Jones."

Feather Jones put her car in gear and turned the corner, pulling up in front of Chez Charming, where Tag Junior asked to meet. Her wealthy clients talked of three-hour lunches here and there was no way she would spend that long with Tug's mortal enemy. Thankfully, a nosey client was coming in for a perm at three p.m. and if Feather rescheduled, she'd want a detailed explanation.

The all-white building with four, tall columns reminded her more of a museum than a place to eat lunch. She felt a knot forming in her stomach, something that was becoming a daily occurrence.

A dour-looking man in a pressed black uniform motioned for her to move forward.

She cracked her window. "Where do I park?"

He viewed her bright-pink-colored hair and dark eyeliner with disapproval. "We park for you, ma'am. This must be your first time here. On this side of town, that's how things are done."

She could feel tension rising inside her already and she hadn't even met Tag Junior yet. The hairs on her arms rose, and soon, a smile crossed her face.

The valet held his hand out, waiting for the keys. He didn't even have the decency to look at her as he waited.

"Your girlfriend dumped you for your roommate? On social media? I can see why you're unhappy."

"What?" His head snapped around. "How did you know that?"

"Those of us on the other side of town pay attention. That's how things are done." She stepped out of her car and handed him the keys. "Make sure it isn't scratched. I'd hate to tell your boss what you told your gaming buddies about his wife."

She walked inside Chez Charming, greeted by the smell of grilled food and expensive perfumes.

"May I help you?" an equally unpleasant woman asked. It must be a theme with the employees. They had to display a certain sour attitude or they weren't hired.

"Yes, I'm here for Tag Muehler. Junior. It's junior and not senior."

The woman raised her eyebrows but made no comment. "Right this way."

She walked slowly, giving Feather the impression she was being paraded in front of the rich people for their amusement. Feather took care to tread as softly as she could in her combat boots, though they made a clomping noise on the shiny wood floor anyway.

They wound their way through the entire restaurant, finally reaching a private booth in the back of the establishment.

The light scent of lilies met her nostrils. There was also a rich, appetizing smell she couldn't define. Whatever it was made her stomach growl.

"Your guest has arrived, Mr. Muehler." The hostess's demeanor changed to one of a woman trying desperately to impress. "May I bring you a drink while you're waiting for your server, miss?"

Feather's mind raced, trying to think of the most expensive drink in her small knowledge base. It wasn't an area of her brain that got much use. "A bubbly water, with lemon please."

She watched the woman walk away before turning to Tag Junior. If she saw him on the street, she'd have no idea he was related to Tug. But now, standing next to him she could see the same wide, expressive eyes and strong chin. They also shared wavy brown hair, but Tag's was cut much shorter than Tug's, giving him a severe, serious look.

"Miss Jones? Glad you could join me." He shook her hand with a smooth, sweaty palm. It wasn't the earnest handshake of Tug, that was for sure.

She looked him in the eye and spoke directly. "Can you tell me why you insisted on me mentoring you? Are you trying to get to Tug?"

"You don't mince words, do you, Miss Jones?"

He took a sip of his mixed drink, no doubt a fancy one he had often, the ice clinking as he set it back down.

She slid into the round booth, unsure how far to move. If she sat too close, she might give him the impression she was interested in him. Too far away and she'd have to strain to hear him. "I'm the newest member of P.I.N.K., so it can't be my experience. And by member, I mean I've been twice. I'm not sure if I'm going to join. They all seemed nice but a little strange.

I'm not used to being around other paranormals. I'm a stylist, that's my day job, and..."

She blushed when she realized she was babbling. It was her go-to when she felt out of place. "It's nice you're concerned about your brother. I've been encouraging him to reconnect, even if it's by text." Her water arrived and she took a sip. The lemon bumped her nose, causing her to gasp and suck in a seed through one of her nostrils.

She looked up at Tag helplessly.

He jumped up and placed his napkin in front of her nose. "Blow harder than you ever have," he instructed. "One...two...three!"

Feather blew with all her might, but nothing happened.

They repeated the process and this time, it produced the offending seed in his napkin.

"Sorry about that," she said sheepishly. "I don't normally inhale my lemons."

Usually, she could go home and laugh about something like this with Tug. It was unfair she didn't have the opportunity to tell him.

Tag smiled, looking relaxed for the first time today. "I raised a son. Food disasters are second nature to me. Now, as we were discussing, I've heard wonderful things about you. Patience Thistle of Thistlewood Manor is in my mother's aqua class. She raves about you all the time."

Feather blushed for the second time. "That's nice of her."

"My mother would like to meet you. The whole family would."

"You haven't mentioned anything about Tug. Would he be included?"

Tag threw his head back and laughed. "Of course. It would be a package deal. We've all missed my brother. He's an integral part of our family. We really thought he'd marry Julianne, but, you know, that fell through."

She felt sick. He was trying to bait her, and it was working. "Who is Julianne?"

"I'm surprised he hasn't told you. When my brother was in high school, he dated a young woman we were all very fond of. They planned to go to college together—she would study architecture and he was going into politics. We were all devastated when it ended."

She decided the best thing would be a change of topic. "What is it you'd like to learn about paranormal investigations?"

"Since discovering I have these abilities, I have been lost. In my world, the ability to do a business deal over lunch is considered an admirable trait. As you can imagine, something like this is thought of as more of a liability. I'd like you to teach me the ropes, as it were."

A large salad was placed in front of Feather. "Oh, no, I didn't–"

"I took the liberty of ordering for you. My sources tell me those are all of your favorite things."

She looked down at the multi-colored work of art;

purple carrots, pickled onions and beets, goat cheese, candied nuts, oranges and several vegetables she didn't recognize. Her stomach rumbled again.

A server brought a large, rare steak and sat it in front of Tag. Definitely not the vegetable-filled plate his brother would have ordered. The only green was a tiny spritz of parsley in the corner.

"If you want me to meet your family, why the big secret about our relationship? Shouldn't you tell Tug? It would be a great icebreaker."

She began munching on the tasty, colorful bowl the size of her head, full of mysterious but wonderful vegetables. The slightly spicy dressing woke tastebuds she didn't know she had.

"Old habits, I guess. We're taught not to trust each other in the Muehler family. I don't want to risk Tug telling the others until I know everything there is to know. Does that make sense?"

Feather nodded, even though she knew Tug was the last person to judge his brother's abilities. "What would you like me to teach you first?"

Tag chewed a large bite of steak and then smiled at her. "This place makes the best steak. You and Tug should try it. I'll leave an anonymous gift certificate at the front for you two."

She resisted the urge to argue that Tug would have many questions about that, starting with, *"Why would some random person do that for us?"*

"I would like to learn how to translate the voices."

"Are they speaking to you in another language? I haven't encountered that before."

She remembered to wipe the corners of her mouth, the way she'd seen actors do in movies.

"No, not that. They're speaking in code. I just don't know what those codes mean."

"Oh, that's pretty normal. I can help you with that. Let's start with the simple stuff. Tell me the words you understand."

Tag took another bite and spoke while he chewed. "Well, I've been warned that someone in my past is trying to hurt me."

"Oh really? Did the spirit give you any more direction?"

"None. That's why I wanted your help."

She took a deep breath. "Let's start with the simple things. Did this spirit give you a name?"

"Oh, yeah," he replied nonchalantly. "He said it was Morgan."

Chapter Eight

GEMINI

"Gemini? Are you alone?"

She lifted herself with care and moved as quickly as she could to the window. She opened it slowly to avoid the weird squeak it made when it went up too fast. Gemini Reed felt like crying when she recognized a familiar face.

One of her best traits was the ability to talk to anyone. During Leo's extended illness, the thing she missed most was a constant companion to share everything with. It was killing her to sit in her room alone. Even on the days when she felt ill and didn't go into the salon, Gemini did crossword puzzles and phoned her friends. Just lying in bed with nothing to do but stare at the ceiling was torturous.

It had been three days since Sergeant Skye assumed command of her home and it already felt endless. Skye helped her out of bed at specified times to walk her around the yard, three times exactly. She helped her to the table for meals, only after Gemini insisted her digestive system couldn't handle sitting in bed to eat, and waited outside the bathroom door while she did her business. It was intolerable.

"The doctor gave none of these instructions when I was released from the hospital," she protested.

"I'm not the doctor, Mrs. Reed. I'm the aftercare specialist and I have my own set of rules." Skye pushed her glasses up her sharp nose and walked out of the room. *Clack clack clack.*

"Tug! You're a sight for sore eyes. I heard your voice last night and was worried that she'd scared you off. You've got to get me out of here. I don't have a phone and Sophia won't be back until next weekend. I'm going crazy," she pleaded.

Tug smiled and reached up to pat her hand reassuringly. "Don't worry, Gem. Your gang is all over this. I've been talking to your neighbor Howard and we have a plan. He's called the exterminator, stating that his rental house is infested with bugs. *U Bug Me* is sending someone in about two hours and Howard has requested a complete sweep of the house. Howard made accommodations for you in his spare room for the duration. You can either stay there and use the phone, or I'll escort you somewhere else."

"That's much appreciated, but Skye will watch me like a hawk."

"Howard requested a call from the state licensing board at the same time. It appears her nursing license is not in order," Tug winked. "It could take an hour or more to fix."

"Oh, dear. I hate to get her in trouble. She's not a bad nurse, she's just not right for me. I don't want her career to suffer."

"Didn't I mention? The call is coming from a retired friend of Howard's who owes him. No real board members contacted. In the meantime, let's get you a better communication device."

Gemini's eyes filled with tears of gratitude. "You boys take such good care of me."

Tug reached up and handed her a burner phone. "Keep this under your bed. I don't know how long it will take to get rid of your nightmare nurse, but in the meantime, you and I can text without her knowing. Feather's worried sick about you, but she's so stressed with her new tasks I don't want her fighting your nurse too."

"What's going on with–"

Tug held up his hand. "She made me promise not to bother you. Once you're sprung from home care permanently, you two can catch up."

"What about your nephew? Were you able to find out anything else about his stay at Smiley Academy?"

"Yes, I found something very interesting."

Gemini heard the familiar click of Skye's heels. She put her finger to her lips and lowered the shade before scurrying back under the covers, placing the phone under her bed as Tug suggested.

The door flew open and Skye breezed in. "It's time for your vitals, Mrs. Reed."

"They've been normal every time you've taken them. When does this end?"

She picked up Gemini's wrist with one hand and made a fist with the other, bringing her watch up to eye level. "When your daughter is satisfied you have recovered sufficiently. Your pulse is a little high today. Maybe I should examine your reading material. It may be causing you unnecessary anxiety."

Gemini scowled at her unreasonable nurse. "I'd like to inform Sophia of my progress. Could I have my phone today? She's got to be worried out of her mind that she hasn't heard from me."

"Pulse is seventy-eight," Skye recited into her phone. "No, your daughter has been kept abreast of the situation. I've explained that you need your rest, and she readily agrees that's the most important thing."

There was no way Sophia would find that excuse reasonable. Skye must've told her something else. "I'd like to at least say hello to my grandson. We talk every Saturday. It's just a few minutes. Nothing taxing."

Skye placed a blood pressure cuff around Gemini's arm and began pumping it. "We'll see. I like my patients to be at eighty percent before they start normal activities."

After dictating Gemini's blood pressure, Skye smiled perfunctorily. "Shall we take your walk around the block? You haven't had bathroom time yet and some exercise will help."

Gemini blushed at the thought of Tug listening to this conversation.

"You don't have to be squeamish, Mrs. Reed. I know people your age are a little old-fashioned about discussing health issues with a professional, but I can assure you, it's perfectly normal. One of my bug-a-boos is dealing with patients who don't believe in total honesty. How am I going to fully assess your situation if you're keeping something from me?"

Gemini swallowed hard. "You know, I believe you're right about my needing extra rest. I think I'd like to take a nap before my walk." Without waiting for Skye's approval, she pulled the covers up to her chin and rolled to her side. "Shut the lights off on your way out, please."

Skye made no effort to move. "But your sched-ule..." She paused.

Gemini imagined the conflict going on in her brain and suppressed a giggle.

"No, you're right, Mrs. Reed. Rest comes before everything. My biggest bug-a-boo is–"

"You can tell me later. I'm much too tired right now."

Her shoes clacking on the polished wood floor, Skye turned out the light and slowly pulled the door shut. Gemini waited, just to make sure there wasn't a last-minute change before throwing the covers back and getting out of bed. She winced as she stood, biting her lip to keep from making any questionable sound.

When she reached the window, she stuck her

head out, gazing down where Tug was squished between a dahlia bush and a miniature pine. Even in this precarious position he was a handsome young man.

"Howard would have a fit if he knew you were traipsing through his plants. What were you telling me about your nephew?"

Tug stood, brushing decorative bark from his shorts. "He was outside the teacher's lounge when a murder occurred. The police questioned him but there's no word whether or not they think he is the killer. It wasn't in any of the papers like you'd think, but in a chat group for the school. It took me over an hour to find it and hack the system."

Gemini gasped. "Who was murdered? I know everyone there."

"Diego Betz. He started this fall as the third-grade teacher. Everyone liked him."

"I've been away too long, it seems. I had no idea they were looking for a new teacher. And who did these people think murdered Mr. Betz?"

"According to the social media page, Rigg heard unfamiliar voices in the room and waited in the hall until they were done arguing. When he walked in the room, he found Mr. Betz lying on the floor. The armchair experts don't believe that. They think Rigg was the killer. If my father hadn't called, I wouldn't have...."

Gemini was utterly shocked. "Smiley Academy has been in existence for a hundred years. Cheese and crackers! I've never heard of anything like that happening before."

"As I mentioned earlier, there is no trace of this murder anywhere. I would almost believe it was just gossip, if I didn't see Smiley Academy advertising for a third-grade teacher, to begin immediately."

"How did he die?"

"A steak knife in the middle of his chest."

The sense of calm she'd felt in speaking with her friend disappeared. There was work to be done and she was unable to help.

She sighed with frustration. "I wish I could get rid of Skye so I can investigate. It sounds like there is some type of coverup and I know just about everyone there. I could question them better than the police."

"Gem, I don't agree with her keeping you locked up, but do you think it's wise to be out of bed and acting like nothing happened? Please don't be offended that I'm asking. I care about you, and I'm just concerned."

"If this were last week, I would agree with you. But it's been two weeks since my surgery and other than an occasional headache and a twinge of abdominal pain, I'm really fine. My arm is healing nicely, and the doctor says I'll be ready for physical therapy by next week." She touched her head, where the stitches were starting to fade. "These things will just dissolve. I don't even think about it. Besides, my brain needs exercising too. It's torturous, lying in bed with nothing to do or think about."

"I can't imagine. I'm so sorry, Gem." Tug was always active, never resting for more than a minute or two before his head hit the pillow at the end of the day. "You and Olive are inspirational. She's a force to be reckoned with too."

"How is Olive doing? Did her wounds heal? I feel terrible about falling on her."

"She's great. Other than a great war story, she's forgotten it happened. She's back at my place now, making this week's order of Tug Bars. We're experimenting with a new flavor that has almond butter, dark chocolate, and crunchy bits of cereal. We don't have a name for it yet, though."

"*'Gem's Favorite'* would be nice," Gemini joked. "I'm so glad you two started working together. And Leo? Did she say how he's doing?"

"Oh, sorry. Olive said he was sitting by the window when she visited him. He frowned when she sat down and the nurse said it was because he didn't recognize her. That's good, right?"

"It's excellent!" In her excitement, Gemini forgot to keep her voiced lowered. She paused just to make sure Skye didn't appear. When nothing happened, she returned to Tug.

"How much time until you bust me out?"

Tug glanced at his watch. "About ninety minutes. You've got a way to contact me now, so don't hesitate to text. My nephew is currently attending school in Charming. I'm going to see if I can communicate with him there."

"Won't the teachers view you as a threat? They call the police nowadays for things like that."

"No, I've come to talk to the kids about nutrition before. They all know me there. The real issue is convincing him I'm his uncle. I haven't seen him since he was a baby."

Skye rapped on the door. "Are you awake? It's almost time for number two."

Gemini shuddered. "Give me a minute. My brain is still foggy."

"Do you remember when you came to visit me in the hospital, and my roommate was forever asking where she was?"

Tug nodded. "Poor lady."

"It turns out, her memory was just fine. She was just used to being the center of attention at her son's house and wanted the same from the hospital staff. All of that confusion was just a performance."

Tug smiled as he pulled a piece of the tree from his hair. "People learn to get attention in whatever way works for them."

"You'll have to do the same with your nephew."

"You can fix this, right?" A new client, Mabel Reynolds, rested her forehead on the wash basin in *Feather Works Salon*, exposing a mismatch of color and dry, knotted hair.

Feather was sickened by the extent of damage Mabel had done to her head. Three different colors of store-bought hair dye, all different shades of red, covered Mabel's scalp. There wasn't an inch of her head that revealed her natural color.

"We only scheduled forty minutes for you today, Mabel, remember? That gives us time to cut and style your hair for your big party tonight." Feather was used to clients making unreasonable demands, but tonight she had another meeting scheduled with Tag Muehler Junior and she couldn't be late. It would take at least three hours to right Mabel's wrongs, and that was without adding new coloring like she asked.

"But I wanted to go to my party tonight as a

blonde! How am I supposed to show up looking like a barber pole?"

Feather massaged her temples, willing the tightness in her chest to go away. "I'm completely booked today, Mabel. If you want to come in next Thursday, I can block off the entire afternoon and we'll get it just the way you want."

Mabel ripped the plastic cape from her body, causing the snaps to fly across the room. She stood menacingly close to Feather's face. "I've never been treated so rudely in all of my years getting my hair colored. The old owner would do whatever I asked. That's your job, isn't it? I'm going to leave a nasty review, warning everyone this salon isn't what it used to be!"

She stomped to the front of the salon, dragging the damaged cape with her. Just as she was about to reach for her purse on the coat hook, she tripped over the cape and went flying into the coat rack. Her nose spurted blood and everyone in the room expelled a collective gasp.

Another customer waiting for an appointment jumped up to help her, but Mabel shoved her away.

"Mabel, let me get some ice for that," Feather offered.

"Do you see what you've done?" Mabel screamed, shoving Feather against the wall. Mabel picked up the last few remnants of the cape and wiped her bloodied face.

Feather made a mental note to thank her new

employee, Stevie-the-new-girl, for the suggestion of buying cheap capes that were easily replaced. Mabel's hands released Feather and she stepped to the side.

She swallowed hard and then looked up at the ceiling, expecting the roof to cave in next. When nothing happened, Feather turned around to see the rest of her staff and customers looking to her for their next move.

"Mabel, I can call a cab for you. I'd feel better about you getting an escort home."

Mabel shook her head. "You've done enough, Feather Jones!" She snapped. As she exited the salon, she took the extra effort to slam the spring-loaded door.

The air left the room with her, until another client got up from her chair and walked over to Feather, opening her arms. Without hesitation, Feather fell against her chest and began to sob.

"It's okay, Feather. Let it out. That was scary for all of us, but no one was at fault."

Stevie-the-new-girl, her newest hire fresh from the beauty school approached Feather timidly. "I still don't have many clients. I'd be happy to take the rest of your appointments for today."

"No, that's okay. I can't just run out–"

"We need you whole and healthy. Please go home and take care of yourself," another stylist, Barb, said. The rest nodded in agreement.

She was shocked to hear such care in the voices of women who had been arguing over nail polish just an hour ago. Shocked and touched.

"I guess I'm outnumbered."

Feather wiped her tears and looked through her bookings, just to make sure she hadn't forgotten anyone. "Two more appointments for today. They're both easy. One is a child's haircut and the other..."

She felt the hairs on her arms rising.

You'll have to wait until I'm alone.

"As I was saying, Stevie-the-new-girl, just two more cuts. I have an appointment later, so I'll leave my phone on, but I am going to rest. Things have been really hectic lately."

When Feather reached her car, she breathed out what could only be described as a complete mental exhaustion. "Okay, what is it?"

Turmoil threatens to explode the portal.

"Morgan, let me explain something. I don't have time to search for portals, let alone portals that explode." She giggled saying that out loud. It sounded ludicrous. After the day she'd had, laughter was the best release.

Turmoil threatens to explode the portal!

"Okay, I get it. I'll be on the lookout. But right now, I'm going to go to the store and find something amazing for dinner. Tug's been working so hard to get his new company off the ground. He needs to see that I can be supportive of him too."

Her phone buzzed. The name on the screen didn't bring any joy to her heart.

"Hi, Tag. What's up?"

She placed one hand on her knee and squeezed as

he spoke, afraid if she let go all of her stored emotions of the day would come pouring out. "Yes, I can meet you there in twenty minutes."

It wasn't exactly what she'd planned to do when she agreed to go home, but it was expected, given the nature of her life recently.

The place Tag Junior chose to meet was an office building on the outskirts of town. Every time she and Tug drove by, she remarked about the beauty of the architecture. The windows had the appearance of being wavy and the building looked like it leaned. Purely an optical illusion. They also noted the fact that the building always appeared deserted.

Suite 440 was on the fourth floor, just past the statue of the first ship captain to drown near Charming. She knocked tenuously on the door, unsure of the proper protocol, and if there were other people inside.

Tag opened the door and ushered her in.

She was surprised to see another familiar face. "Mr. Beasley? What are you doing here?"

He smiled and adjusted his pink cape. "It's Capu when we're talking business. It's nice to see you again, Feather."

The fact that he was wearing his strange cape in public was another big strike against the P.I.N.K. organization. There was no way she'd be caught wearing that thing around town.

"Sorry, Capu. When Tag Junior said it was an emergency, I thought he was having some kind of crisis. If you're here, he won't need my help."

"I asked him to call. It's a little naughty of me, but I set you up. I wanted you to come for your session so I could watch your methodology. You're still in the probationary period."

Feather's face burned. She hadn't asked to join them, they asked her. She didn't have time for silly tests, or Tag Junior for that matter. But she'd made a promise to Jayden. If she was being honest, a small part of her was also curious about Tug's brother. Maybe through him, she would gain more perspective on her boyfriend.

"Okay, what's the test?"

"You need to guide Tag Junior as he communicates with the spirit presence. Tag tells me he's been getting messages from someone called Morgan."

She nodded and studied Tag Junior's face. He took a sip of his cocktail, the same color as the one he drank at Chez Charming, and looked the other way.

"Well then, Mr. Muehler, I'd like you to summon this Morgan fellow and let Feather talk you through your visit." Mr. Beasley sat down on a pea-green sofa and fluffed his cape beside him.

Tag Junior smiled slightly. Feather wasn't sure if he was amused or annoyed.

"I'll try. Feather has told me these things don't always happen on the living's timeline. Are you ready, Miss Jones?"

"Go for it," she replied without enthusiasm.

Tag Junior closed his eyes and rolled his head back,

something she hadn't observed him doing before. He moaned softly and mouthed words.

"Morgan says you've been receiving messages about a teacher at my son's school."

"Me?" In this unexpected turn of events, Feather was caught completely unaware. "I don't...give me a minute."

She sat down and cleared her head, hoping there was someone available who might talk to her. Anger pushed at the corners of her chest, and she felt stinging needles of pain. She wasn't a trained monkey, and she wasn't about to pretend she could summon spirits at the drop of a hat.

Turmoil threatens to explode the portal.

Feather frowned and shook her head.

"Are you getting anything yet?" Tag Junior asked impatiently.

"No, nothing at all." She opened her eyes. "If you'll give me more time–"

"It's not up to Feather to determine your messages, Mr. Muehler. Feather, explain to him how he can interpret the message himself."

Tag closed his eyes again, this time, nodding furiously. "Okay, yes, yes. Thank you, Morgan."

A memory popped into her head. On their eighteen-month anniversary, Tug took her to the Charming Dinner Theatre. She'd never been to a live theatrical performance before and she studied the actors with curiosity. Their over-pronunciation of words and exaggerated hand movements stuck with her.

Tag Muehler Junior was exhibiting the same characteristics. He was acting. Whether it was for Capu or for her, she wasn't sure. It was pure performance art.

"What did you hear?" Feather asked. "Explain to me what this experience tells you."

"Morgan wants you to investigate Smiley Academy. He says their practices are suspect and a killer is among them. He's sure you'll solve this mystery."

"Oh my, that sounds intriguing!" Mr. Beasley remarked. "I hadn't read anything in the news about a murder, it must've just happened. That's far beyond the capabilities I'd assumed you possessed, Mr. Muehler. Good job, both of you!" Mr. Beasley jumped up and shook both of their hands. Agility was something she didn't think he was capable of, given the endless afternoons he sat on the porch immobile.

"Keep up the good work. I think I can schedule your initiations for next week."

"Next week?" they asked in unison.

"I didn't know anything about an initiation," Feather grumbled. "I'm not interested in drinking funny things or walking on hot coals. Jayden promised me there would be no hazing stuff."

"Oh, it won't be anything like that. We'll just need a display of your skills."

"Not mine!" Tag retorted. "I'm just here to learn. I never said anything about joining the group! If you want my funding, you'll have to follow my rules."

Mr. Beasley didn't seem at all offended, at least that

was what he portrayed. "Either way, you'll both be expected to attend. If you use our services, it's required that you join, no matter what you donate. I'll be taking my leave now. I like to watch the rush hour traffic."

"I need to go too. I have to get to the store..."

Tag Junior grabbed Feather's arm. "Wait, please."

She shook free but stood in place until Mr. Beasley was gone.

"What?" She no longer felt she had to jump through hoops. Tag Muehler Junior was a fraud. It was just a matter of finding the right moment to confront him.

"You don't have to worry about an initiation. I'm giving this group a large sum of money, which is contingent on my satisfaction."

"What kind of satisfaction are you looking for?" Her eyes narrowed with suspicion. Now he was going to ask her for the impossible—make Tug come work for them at Muehler Enterprises. It had been there in front of her all along.

Tag leaned his body towards her, and she tensed, ready to strike if necessary.

"The fulfillment of my contract with this group. Finding out what these messages mean. If you were thinking of something else, then you're mistaken," he replied in a calm voice. "You're not my type."

Chapter Ten

GEMINI

"Gemini Reed, rumor had it you were confined to a wheelchair!" Olive grabbed her weak body and hugged it with a robustness Gemini wasn't ready for.

"I'm glad to see you too, Olive." She pulled herself away from her friend and into Tug and Feather's apartment.

Their escape had gone according to plan. The exterminator showed up at the door, insisting he was there at the behest of the landlord and there was nothing Skye could do about it.

Howard came soon after and assured Skye it was necessary. He said he'd take Gemini to his home and show her to his guest room. "You're welcome to come too, Ms. Baker."

Skye was on their heels as they made the transfer, that is until her phone rang. Gemini squeezed

Howard's arm, knowing it was the fake mix-up with Skye's credentials.

"I'm just a phone call away. Your personal car service. We should head back in an hour or so. Your nurse will break down my door if I keep you away longer than that," Howard called. He'd escorted her to Feather's door, ignoring Gemini's insistence she was fine walking on her own.

As much as it irritated her that she was being treated like a breakable vase, she had to admit, it was nice to have friends willing to help when she needed it. "Thanks, Howard."

Olive stuck her head out the door and called, "You can stay, Howard. We've got plenty of room."

When he didn't reply, she shrugged and closed the door. "That neighbor of yours is a silver fox, Gemini. One of these days, I'm going to tame that man with my cooking."

She nodded, not energetic enough to convince Olive otherwise.

"It smells wonderful in here, Olive! What are you baking?"

Gemini moved to the kitchen, where bars sat on cooling racks. Dozens more had been iced in a zig-zag fashion with chocolate. She maneuvered gently onto a kitchen stool.

Olive put her hands on her large hips and chuckled. "Today's masterpieces are Gem's Favorite. A little birdie told me you'd like them. Would you like to try one?"

"I'd love one! I haven't eaten anything of my own choosing since I went into the hospital. Oh, did someone pick up my container from the salon? You know how people like to scoop those up."

"Already took it over to your place. You were sleeping that day."

It was more likely she was locked away in her bedroom, but explaining that would require too much effort.

"I'd like to go to the Smiley Academy and let them think I'm ready to rejoin the board. Though the staff and board members are tight-lipped around parents, they are a gossipy group when they are alone."

Gemini sat back uneasily, experiencing more pain and fatigue. She would never hear the end of it if Skye discovered she was right about taking it easy.

"That would be a wonderful idea any other time, Gemini," Tug said, pulling up a stool beside her. "But you're not ready for that kind of activity. I think I should go in. I'll pretend I'm enrolling my son." His knee bounced up and down, the cadence matching his exuberant speech pattern. "I've always wanted to name a boy Dagg."

"That's not gonna work." Olive walked over to the window, where two boisterous children played on the communal deck of the apartment building across the street. "What if your nephew is the spitting image of you? We can't take that chance. From what Gemini tells us, they may be gossips but they aren't stupid."

Gemini cleared her throat. "But they've never seen Rigg's grandmother, have they?"

"How would that benefit us, Gem?" Tug asked. "I'm not opposed, I just don't understand how it will help."

"During my tenure on the board, a child was kicked out for filling up the toilet with the soapy water used to clean paint brushes. It overflowed and made quite the colorful mess." She chuckled, remembering how Leo was called in for a consultation on ridding the place of paint. He replied he didn't see anything wrong with a multi-colored bathroom. *"The color scheme worked well, actually brightened up the place!"*

"The boy swore he didn't do it, but the principal was adamant he couldn't come back," she continued. "Then, his grandma came for a visit and everything changed. The principal is a great fan of family matri-archs, at least that's what the rumor was. I think there's more truth in the idea that she follows the trail of money. After that visit, her grandson moved back into the dorm with no further punishment."

"I'll go as Rigg's grandma. I'll ask for a tour and pump her for information on Mr. Betz's death. Then, with the help of your bank account, I'll grease a few palms." Olive rubbed her hands together. "I'm getting good at this detective stuff."

"Olive, are you sure you want to put yourself in that position?"

It wasn't physical pain she was feeling at that

moment, it was jealousy. This was the kind of case that got her juices flowing.

"I'll put a recording device on your shirt like I did when you went to the Daymont mansion. I can even find an earpiece so I can talk to you." Tug stood and paced excitedly. "This could work. Olive, your eyes and ears have to be open. That means looking at every minute detail while the principal is talking." Tug paused to gaze at Gemini, whose smile was anything but genuine.

"Gemini, since you're familiar with Fassetville, could you call the police department and get the police report? And I'll search obituaries and see if I can find one for him and any next-of-kin."

She nodded. "Of course. I've spoken with them about cases many times. They know me well."

"We're quite the team, aren't we?" Tug smiled at his friends. "I don't think there's any case we can't solve."

"Gemini? You're looking pale. Do you want to lie down?" Olive placed her hand on Gemini's back and stared intently into her face. "I don't want a repeat of our last time together!"

"Yes, I might do that. I've never apologized for causing your stitches, Olive. I am sorry for my collapse at your expense."

Olive smiled, her eyes bright and lively. "That was the most excitement we had in the Charming Acres Retirement Facility in months. Everyone stopped by to bring me a casserole or cookies. Even the staff came over. One nice man brought flowers too. You can knock me over any time!"

Tug chuckled. "Olive, if you started dating, we'd never get our Tug Bars work finished!"

"Could someone tell Howard I'll be a bit longer? I don't know what we'll tell Skye. If she knocks on the door to Howard's guest room and I don't answer, she'll decide I've fallen into a coma."

Tug picked up his phone. "I'm calling Howard now. Let us take care of your nurse. Go get some rest. Oh, and I'll bring in my new invention—Olive You Feels Great. It's an energy drink Olive helped me test. I think you'll like it."

"It had me jumping around like a frog in a pan the first time I tasted it," Olive added. She took Gemini's arm and helped her to her feet. "Now I can't wait to drink some every morning. It's going to be a big hit, I can tell!"

Though she hated being treated like an invalid, the cool quiet of Feather and Tug's bedroom soothed her. It wasn't the prison her room had become, it was a friendly place with a door that opened both ways. She drank the entire glass of green juice Olive brought her and fell asleep. When she awoke, Feather was sitting beside the bed.

"Feather? Gracious, dear. I've missed you so much! How are you?"

Feather leaned in close and took her hand. "I've missed you too, friend."

There was a quiet in the room that was unusual. "Tell me."

"Tell you what, Gemini?"

"I need to know what's troubling you. Tug is beside himself with worry and you know I'll never fully recover until I know my friend is all right."

Feather's eyes filled with tears, an unusual display of emotion for someone who prided herself on her lack of drama.

"Gemini, I've got myself mixed up in something, and I don't know how to get out."

"This is my strongest super power. My ears are ready, and my heart is open."

"That's the thing, I'm not supposed to tell anyone. P.I.N.K. has convinced me that they have magic powers or some kind of voodoo that allows them to see into my mind. It's got me looking over my shoulder all the time and I'm becoming one of those weird, paranoid types."

"Cheese and crackers! That's tough." Gemini pushed herself up to a sitting position. "What if you told me the story using different names? Tell me what Gemini and Howard did in their Iris Club."

"I don't know...what if..." She nodded with vigor. "You're right, as always. I need to get this off my chest or I think I'm going to explode."

"I shall clear my mind of any thoughts of you and your group." Gemini closed her eyes and took a few deep breaths. "Now, you may proceed."

"Okay. 'Gemini' was invited to join the Iris Club,

but it turned out it was more of a demand than a request. Apparently, her iris-growing skills are better than most."

"I told her she was good at her job!" Gemini said enthusiastically. "So far, it doesn't sound bad."

"As a part of her initiation, she was required to tutor another member. A new member who is... disagreeable. Let's say it's Howard's brother."

"Tug's brother? Rigg's father? He's...Tug's brother is a clairvoyant?"

Feather nodded, forgetting her insistence on discretion. "He's just awful. He's the exact opposite of my good and kind boyfriend, even though he wants me to think he's perfect. And he's just pretending to have a gift. Tag follows my lead more than anything. He's got some other reason for being there. Maybe he still thinks I'm after his brother for his inheritance."

"Can you tell them you want to mentor another iris grower?"

Feather shook her head. "Mr. Bee..." she paused before she gave away the biggest secret of all, that Gemini's neighbor was the de facto leader of P.I.N.K. "The Iris Club leader is insistent I tutor this person. I've recently come to believe that Howard's brother is, in fact, a fraud. He has no skills at all. The worst part is that if I leave, Howard's brother won't give the sizeable donation he promised to the organization, and they may have to disband."

"Cheese and crackers! You've got a burden the size

of a car on your shoulders!" Gemini rubbed Feather's hand. "I'm sorry, sweetie. That's too much."

"I'm stuck, Gem. I don't know what to do or how to remove myself. If I just walk away, they'll ruin my reputation."

The door opened and Tug entered, carrying a tray with vegetable soup and more of his green drink. "We worked everything out with your prison guard. Provided we feed you what she wanted and let you rest."

"She convinced you to feed me gruel?"

The wonderful smell filling the room would say otherwise, but Gemini couldn't pass up the opportunity to tease Tug.

"No, this is soup I made for us last night. Feather was running late with her club," Tug glanced sideways, "and I had lots of leftovers."

Feather looked pleadingly at Gemini.

"She's been telling me how thinly stretched she is lately. What with the loss of help at the salon and the secret responsibilities in her new group. And you have this business taking off, Tug. The two of you need to give each other a break."

He set the tray on her bed and hugged Feather. She reached up and kissed him deeply.

"Oh, my. This soup is divine!" Gemini spooned the rich broth into her mouth. "Tug, I must get your recipe. Beyond that, I have to tell you, I believe your miracle drink has renewed my energy."

"You'll be back to your old self in no time, Gem." Feather took a napkin and gently wiped the sides of her friend's mouth.

"Is Olive all set for her undercover work?"

"She's bursting at the seams with excitement."

Chapter Eleven

GEMINI

"Feather was called away at the last minute. I hope you don't mind, I'm her replacement."

Gemini adjusted her body in the oddly shaped chair. She was feeling much better, but there were still instances where she was reminded of her recent surgery. "I got special permission from my home nurse to come today. She won't let me drive yet, but just going out the front door without her giving me the evil eye is progress like you can't imagine."

"Mrs. Reed, your neighbor is a powerful man. He says he can get me a job at the hospital in Piney Falls if I follow his directive with you. I'm torn, I am working for your daughter after all. But he's promised to get me on the surgical floor. That's where the big money is."

Howard sat in his vehicle in front of the massive, three-story structure where Tag Muehler Junior made his home. It was sometimes easy to forget that Tug came from such wealth. He was the humblest being she knew.

Gemini waved to him as the door opened and found herself inside a showpiece that resembled those in the magazines in her doctor's waiting room. Their shoes echoed through the massive space as he guided her to a pair of white couches.

She lowered herself carefully, expecting the best comfort of her life but instead finding a rock-hard seat.

"What brings you today, Mrs. Reed?" His shoulders were so tight they hovered underneath his ears.

Gemini frowned. "Don't you know why I'm here? We're discussing your son."

Tag Muehler Junior relaxed. "Oh, that's right. Miss Jones and I have other business. Can I get you something to drink? I have tea and soda. My maid is off today, or I'd offer you coffee. She's mastered all of the buttons on that machine and keeps promising to give me a tutorial."

"Tea would be fine. While you're in the kitchen, I'd like you to think on something for me."

Tag stood, his muscular body resembling his brother's, though if there was a contest, Tug would win for overall definition.

"What is that?"

"I'd like to know who at the Smiley Academy has a vendetta against the Muehler family. I used to be on the board and don't remember your family name ever being discussed."

"I–"

Gemini put her finger to her lips. "Not now. Think about it and we'll discuss it when you come back. I'd love a nice chamomile if you have it."

When Tug exited the living room, she looked around for any obvious clues about his lifestyle. An intricately-carved wooden fixture hung behind the television set. There was a cabinet made out of matching wood sitting directly underneath the television. She wondered if she'd have time to move to that side of the room and examine it before Tag returned.

"Ummph." Extracting herself from the couch wasn't as difficult as she'd assumed. "All right, Skye. Those torturous exercises you make me do every day are paying off. You win this round."

She opened the top drawer of the cabinet carefully and was surprised to see a framed wedding photo sitting on top of lots of papers. It was Tag's wedding day. His wife was dressed as though she'd just walked out of Brides Monthly. Her veil was so long, three children were holding it off the ground.

Scanning the large group, she found Tug in the back. He was wearing a groomsman's tuxedo, but unlike the other groomsmen, he was not smiling. They looked like frat boys, each with an arm draped across the next. All except Tug. His arms were stiff at his sides and for the first time since she'd known him, Gemini realized he wasn't smiling.

Gemini lifted the photo and found several baby

pictures of Rigg. At each stage of his toddlerhood, he wore the same tiny cross necklace around his neck.

She put them away and picked up the wedding photo again, moving from groomsman to groomsman. She gasped when she came to the fourth groomsman. "Cheese and crackers!"

"Planning a wedding? My wedding to Martine was the best and worst day of my life."

He set the tea down and walked over to her, seemingly not upset about her snooping.

"What makes it so? I understand it's the best, but why the worst?" Gemini asked.

"I'm sure my brother has filled you in on all the sordid details of our family. I don't need to rehash the end of my marriage." He crossed his arms and stepped aside. "Would you like your tea now?"

The thought of returning to that uncomfortable couch made her cringe. "Maybe I'll stand and drink it. I've spent far too much time in bed. Would you mind?"

Tag handed her a tall mug with "Proud Dad" painted across the side. "My wedding was also the worst day for me. Martine wasn't the woman she portrayed herself to be. After giving birth to our son, she insisted on separate vacations. At first, I thought it was a normal thing. You know, a new mother needing her space. But then I found out my uncle was taking vacations at the very same time. Martine and Uncle Chugg were having an affair. When I confronted her, she moved out overnight. She's never called once to check on her son."

"I'm so sorry to hear that. Your brother never breathes a word about your family's troubles. In fact, until your nephew had his tragic accident, I didn't even know Rigg existed."

"Humph," Tag snorted. "That figures. He's never tried to be one of us. He rejected our company. I can't tell you the last time he joined us for a holiday."

"You can't have it both ways, Tag." Gemini took another sip. "This is very good tea. I'll have to get the brand name."

"What do you mean?"

"I mean, you and your family push him away and tell him he's different, but then demand he partake in your activities? Does that make sense to you?"

Tag shrugged. "I guess when you put it that way, no it doesn't. But now he's got himself involved with Miss Jones. He's never been wise about who he spends time with. I think she's after his money."

Knowing that Feather was forced to hide her inter-actions with Tag from her boyfriend, Gemini fought to control her anger. "You have the means to do a back-ground check on Feather. I'm sure if you had, you would realize she doesn't have a dishonest bone in her body. She is my closest friend, and I'll thank you to keep your ugly thoughts out of our conversation!"

Tag looked away. "What was it you wanted to know again?"

"I'm here about your son. I've yet to find evidence

he killed that teacher, but there have been many suspicious events surrounding his death. Did your son have issues with Professor Betz?"

"He didn't even have any classes with him. The first day of school, parents all came to the opening convocation. I'm sure he was there, but I don't remember any interactions with him. Rigg swears he didn't know him and didn't have any reason to harm him."

"Did your son have any acquaintances who didn't like him? Maybe someone who thought pinning a murder on Rigg would remove him from their lives?"

Tag shook his head. "My son isn't always open with me, so I can't say for sure, but he's a nice kid. He's never met anyone he can't strike up a friendship with."

Just like his Uncle Tug.

"Have the police contacted you about the investigation?"

"That's the funny thing. Since that first night, when they arrested him, they haven't said or done anything. I talked to our lawyer just this morning. He thought it was odd too that he'd not heard anything."

"I'm going to look into this further. Believe it or not, your brother would like me to clear his nephew's name."

Tag tried unsuccessfully to stifle a giggle. "How would you clear his name? No offense, Mrs. Reed, but–"

"But you don't find me capable? I won't bore you with listing the crimes I've solved in this community, but I would like to ask you one simple question."

"Okay, I'm sorry. That was rude of me. If my brother thinks you can solve this thing, then more power to you. What would you like to ask?"

Gemini walked over to the drawer and removed the wedding photo, holding it beside her head.

"Why is the murder victim in your wedding photo? Groomsman number four, if I counted correctly."

Chapter Twelve

FEATHER

Stevie-the-new-girl approached Feather cautiously. She stood slightly out of Feather's reach, twiddling her thumbs as she waited for a pause in the light banter between Feather and her client, Donna.

"Stevie-the-new-girl, you'll learn that we don't stand on ceremony here." Feather took a piece of Donna's dull brown hair and expertly wrapped it tightly around a blue perm roller.

"Feather's Salon is like my extended family gatherings. You either spit it out, or you'll lose the chance to talk at all," Donna added.

Stevie-the-new-girl tapped her foot quickly and her eyes darted back and forth. "I...um...it's just that you've been so stressed lately, I don't want to add to your problems."

Feather set her comb down on the metal stand she used to hold all of her supplies and took Stevie-the-new-girl's hands. "I was timid like you when I started. I just assumed everyone else knew more than me. When I finally decided I belonged here, just like every other stylist, my life went much better. Own it, sister."

Stevie-the-new-girl nodded, though she still appeared uneasy.

"Now, I want you to pull your shoulders back, set your feet wide, and own your space." Feather showed her how it was done, stomping her combat boots as she moved her feet into place. "See? No one's going to mess with me now."

Stevie-the-new-girl did as instructed and gave Feather a half-smile.

"I can see you're not completely onboard. That's okay, it can take time to claim your own ground. Tell me whatever it is and say it with confidence. I can take it." Feather winked at Donna in the mirror.

Stevie-the-new-girl's mouth moved but nothing came out.

"Louder, Stevie-the-new-girl."

"You've got this, girl!" Donna encouraged.

"The plumber called and said the leaking pipes are caused by the city's upgrade to its sewer system. It will cost five thousand dollars to change all of your pipes to bring them up to the new codes."

Stevie-the-new-girl's posture remained stiff.

"What else?"

"While I was taking down the information, someone else beeped in. Mabel Reynolds, the woman who wanted you to fix her hair before her party, has retained a lawyer. She's suing you for assault."

Donna gasped. "Don't worry, honey. Your insurance company will pay her, that's why you have them. But then they'll drop you."

Feather could feel her insides tightening again. "Was that it?"

"Yes," Stevie-the-new-girl shook her head. "You're right though, it felt good to tell you with confidence."

Feather smiled weakly and nodded. "Donna, I need a breath of fresh air. I'll be right back." She remembered Donna mentioned she had another appointment at 3:30. She looked up at the clock and saw to her dismay, it was 2:20 and her perm would require at least another hour.

"Stevie-the-new-girl, could you finish rolling Donna's hair? All of the perm rods are right here."

She didn't wait for Stevie-the-new-girl's reply, instead racing towards the back door to the alley.

Leaning up against her building she put her hands on her knees and tried to calm the storm that was raging inside her. The hairs on her arms rose.

"Not now!" She screamed, causing the pigeons eating a soggy cookie to fly off.

The sensation of unwelcome guests in her head didn't dissipate like it usually did when she was firm.

Turmoil threatens to explode the portal
The house of turns is a façade
Find the sheep made of iron

She clapped her hands over her ears and sunk to the ground. "I can't do this!"

Her chest tightened again, this time restricting

oxygen so severely she could barely breathe. Feather fell to the ground, resting her head on the grimy surface. Nothing on her wanted to move.

After what felt like hours, she heard the door open. "Feather? I've got her processing. Is there anything else you..." Stevie-the-new-girl knelt down by her side and took her pulse. "Your heart is racing. Is the pain in your chest?"

Feather nodded slowly. "I can't breathe," she whispered.

"I'm going to yell for someone to call 9-1-1 and then I'll stay here by your side."

She rose and opened the door, yelling in a loud but calm voice, "We need an ambulance."

The other two women working that day rushed to the door and then sat beside Feather.

"Is this because I wanted a raise?" Lisa asked. "I'm sorry. You can't afford it. That was really stupid."

Feather tried to protest but Stevie-the-new-girl pressed her finger to Feather's lips. "Don't talk. Just rest until the medics arrive." She turned to Lisa. "Get her on her back with her feet propped up. I volunteered as a candy striper for the hospital one summer and we had to learn first aid."

"Should we move her inside?" Lisa asked.

"No, we don't know what other injuries she might have. She's staying right here." The shy, unsure-of-herself-Stevie-the-new-girl from earlier disappeared, replaced by a confident woman who knew how to handle an emergency.

"I had this happen once. It was after my parents divorced and my brother wouldn't speak to anyone. The doctor said the only medication I needed was a week away from my family," another stylist added, somewhat unhelpfully.

Feather tried desperately to talk, but her voice had disappeared.

"What is it, Feather? Are you having pain somewhere else?" Stevie-the-new-girl-the-new-girl bent down next to Feather's head, her long, blonde and brown hair dropping into Feather's mouth.

Stevie-the-new-girl sat up and frowned for a moment. "Oh, she wants us to call Tug. Would you do that, Lisa?"

"On it." Lisa disappeared inside.

By the time the ambulance arrived, Tug had as well. He rubbed her back until the EMTs placed her body on a stretcher. When she saw him, she felt even worse. There was nothing more gut-wrenching to her than the concern all over his face.

"I'm here, Feath."

Stevie-the-new-girl-the-new-girl stepped out of the way and he grabbed Feather's hand, bringing it to his lips. "I'm riding with you to the hospital. I've already worked it out with the EMTs."

"I'm here too, dear." She recognized Olive's voice.

"Tug asked if I'd stick around and make sure everything gets locked up and the lights are out at the end of the day," Stevie-the-new-girl-the-new-girl announced as Feather was being loaded into the ambulance. "I know the alarm code and I'll make sure all the cash goes to the bank. Don't worry about anything, Feather. I know what to do."

"I'll stay too," Olive chimed in. "Tug says I'm a greater help right here than at the hospital."

Feather's mouth turned upward, all the smile she could muster right now. Tug knew how Olive would get in the way at the hospital, so he'd found another place she would feel needed.

As she was being wheeled into the exam room, Feather drifted in and out, suddenly very sleepy. She could make out familiar voices of entities who watched over her. They were concerned, too, sending her their energy.

Feather drifted into blissful sleep with Tug at her side, holding her hand. It was the best, dreamless sleep she'd had in months.

After what seemed like hours and many tests, the doctor came in.

He walked with a bounce in his step and Feather wondered for a moment if this was his demeanor no matter what the diagnosis.

"You suffered what we call an anxiety attack. It can mimic a heart attack in symptoms. What we'll need for you, young lady, is to do a deep dive—that's what the kids call it right?" He paused and when neither of them answered, he continued. "Yes, a deep dive into your life.

No more stress, or at least the stressors you can control. While this wasn't a full-blown heart attack, it serves as a good warning system that your body has reached its limits."

He looked over at Tug. "You, young man, need to step in whether she asks or not. I have a feeling your girlfriend isn't one to ask for back up."

Tug winked at Feather. "You have no idea, sir."

"I'll have a nurse come in with follow-up instructions, and hope I don't see you again." He walked toward the door but pivoted back, bouncing to the bed. "Just a few words of wisdom from my own marriage. If you're keeping things from each other, don't. That small act is like carrying a twenty-pound sack on your back. Good luck, Miss Jones."

Feather couldn't bring herself to meet Tug's gaze. She felt as though she was a child again, facing her parents with yet-another disappointing report card.

The doctor bounced back in through the door for a third time, before either of them had composed themselves. "I had a lightbulb moment. That's what the kids say, right? I want you, young man, to set a timer on that fancy sports watch of yours. Set it for ten minutes and I'll make sure no one comes in to bother you during that time."

He glanced over at Feather, peering at her over the top of his dark-rimmed glasses. "And you, young lady, I want you to leave everything here on the emergency room floor. Don't save anything for later. Pretend I just did surgery to remove your stressors. You don't want to carry them back home again, do you? Use this time wisely. It's my gift to you. There's only one rule. When you get home, there will be no judgments, nor will there be repercussions. You'd be surprised how many people have done that and seen remarkable changes in their health."

He walked out the door, calling back, "Ten minutes. No holds barred."

Once they were sure he was gone, for good this time, Tug set his watch to ten beeps and then squeezed Feather's hand. "Since we're leaving it all on the floor... There is something that's been bothering me, Feath. Are you cheating on me?"

"What?" She couldn't fathom why he'd get that idea. Ever since they'd met, she was completely devoted to Tug Muehler, the most perfect soul she'd ever met. "Of course not! There is only one man for me, Tug Muehler!"

The thought of him anguishing over a supposed other relationship hurt her heart. The doctor's plan was having the opposite effect.

"Then what is it, Feather? You've been holding everything inside. We're partners, we share in life equally."

She thought about her promise to keep Tag Junior's gifts a secret and his threat to pull the funding if she didn't comply with his wishes. Jayden would be angry that she shared with Tug. "I know about your high school girlfriend. How she was the love of your life."

Tug dropped her hand. "How did you find out about Julianne?"

"Later. Tell me about her. Are you two still talking?"

Tug's eyes widened. "She's dead. About fourteen years ago." He crossed his arms and walked over to the window. He turned the upper half of his body towards her. "And no, she was most certainly not the love of my life. That role will always be filled by one Feather Jones."

If it were possible, she loved him even more at that moment.

"We were high school sweethearts. She was cute and stubborn. I guess I have a type." He chuckled softly.

"When we graduated, she wanted to go to the college her parents chose for her. I refused to go to my dad's alma mater. I didn't want to go anywhere. I've already told you about the dark depression I was in for years."

Feather nodded, tears forming in the corners of her eyes.

"At first, we'd get together when she was home on breaks, but it became apparent that our lives had taken two completely different turns. We never agreed to stay together, by then we were just meeting because it seemed like the right thing to do. One Easter she came home and didn't call. I wasn't sad, I was actually relieved I didn't have to put on a pretend happy face for her. She had no tolerance for my depression, and I had little understanding for someone who wasn't unhappy."

"Oh, Tug. I'm sorry. That must've been painful."

He shook his head vehemently. "That's what I'm telling you—it wasn't. I was beyond feeling anything for anyone. I saw her mother once and she accidentally let it slip that Julianne was dating someone in college. She thought it would upset me, but I couldn't have cared less."

"How did she..."

"Die? I was getting treatment for my depression. I was at the most expensive facility in Portland my family could find. That meant they were also the most discreet. That was the real reason they chose it." Tug laughed. "Yes, my family is so predictable. Always spending money for the benefit of their own needs."

Feather swallowed hard. "Did the staff tell you she was gone?"

"No, it was my mother. She came up for the afternoon. You should've seen her, Feath. She was wearing this ridiculous blonde wig and big glasses. If her goal was to appear discreet, it didn't happen."

Feather had only seen pictures of Tug's mother. She didn't look friendly. In fact, her face looked frozen in a permanent grimace. Feather always assumed that was a request she made of her plastic surgeon.

"Mom came up that day and said I should call her Aunty Marion, just to make sure no one thought she might be my mother. I said okay, and then she said, 'Your poor girlfriend found tragedy. She was out for a run and a drunk driver hit her. The poor girl had such potential. That the two of you would end up like this is a real tragedy.' "

"Oh, Tug. That's how she thought it should come out?"

"That's my mother for you. It was several months before I was out of the facility. By then, her funeral had taken place and life moved on. I wasn't eager to return to my darkness, so I didn't allow myself to think about it. My Uncle Chugg, who was estranged from the family, called me twice, asking if I'd like to talk about her. He was a mentor for Julianne in college and he said they were close. He asked more than once if I wanted to talk about her, and I always said no."

"I'm so sorry. Even if you weren't close at the time, that had to hurt."

Tug returned to her side and picked up her hand again. "Feath, is that all you want to leave here?"

She thought again about her commitment to Tag Junior. He was a farce. Something was still preventing her from telling Tug. Maybe she didn't want him to feel the added rejection that was sure to come.

"That's it, Tug. That's all I had."

Chapter Thirteen

GEMINI

"I'm going on record to say that I strongly disagree with you leaving the house without me." Skye folded her arms across her chest. "Your landlord ambushed me, and I don't appreciate it."

Gemini shrunk into her bed.

I'll pick you up in twenty minutes. Can you handle Nurse Nightmare?

"I'm feeling more energized every day, thanks to your expert care, Skye."

The doorbell rang and Skye frowned. "I thought we were done with strangers."

"You'd better answer it. The people delivering my medication won't just leave it by the door."

Gemini waited for the clacking of Skye's heels before she pulled the covers back, revealing her favorite lemon-yellow pants and top. She was pleased by how smoothly she was able to get out of bed today, with just a twinge of pain. After running the brush through

99

her hair, she applied a coat of Pink Persimmon on her lips.

Howard Beachmont smiled with satisfaction. "You've done an excellent job getting our Gemini back on her feet, Ms. Baker. Now It's time for her to give them a test run. I'll be with her the whole time. If anything goes wrong, it will rest squarely on my shoulders."

Skye held her ground. "This is an outrage! Her time at your home was too much for my patient. She's still weak and in her bed, barely able to–"

"I'm ready, Howard."

Skye pivoted, clearly shocked by Gemini's appearance. "What are you doing out of bed?"

Howard brushed by her and offered his hand to his friend. "Are you ready?"

"Looking forward to this for hours now." She tried tamping her excitement down for Skye's sake, but it felt good to be out without restrictions.

"I'll be back soon. You can check every inch of me when I return, I promise."

Skye, still stunned by the turn of events, didn't respond until they were in the car.

"This is unacceptable!" She yelled. "One of my biggest bug-a-boos is a patient who refuses to..." her voice trailed off as they turned the corner.

When she was out of sight, they both let out a big sigh of relief.

"I feel like I've broken out of prison for the second

time. There's a small touch of regret, but a whole big feeling of freedom."

"Don't know if I would have chosen her for this job," Howard remarked. "She needs a patient who is unconscious."

"I feel the same way. This must be my son-in-law's way of getting back at me. We're in a constant tug-of-war for my daughter's affections." It was time to change the subject, before she let her emotions pull her into a dark space. "Will we have time to visit Leo? Did you time this out for us?"

"Down to the second. You know me, Gemini. I like planning."

They sped down the road toward Feather's apartment. "After Leo's experience, I told myself I'd never forget to feel gratitude. But looking at these luscious trees and the sunshine, I realize I've done just that. Even the air smells different when it's been forbidden."

"If I didn't know any better, Gemini Reed, I'd say you were downright happy." Howard's lips curled into a smile. "It's good to see you relaxed after your ordeal."

"Fill me in now. I know the kids do all of their communication via text, but my fingers don't move that fast. I gave up trying to message with Tug, anything other than the basics. What is our plan today?"

"We're meeting Mr. Muehler's nephew at a playground. Or rather, you are. My next assignment is to wait until you text me that you're ready to come home. I'll be in the coffee shop."

"Now you're teasing me, Howard."

"Tug's nephew has Tae Kwon Do at two. When he's finished, he's agreed to meet you for thirty minutes. At that point, I'll take him home and drop him off precisely one block from his house so his parents will think he walked."

"I don't know how you managed to finagle this, Howard. Did Tug contact you? Or are you just that good at reading my mind?"

"You know I have sources everywhere. I was able to get word to Rigg via a teacher at Charming High School. She was a patient at the hospital when I was there and owed me a favor. I asked Tug's permission before setting up your date. We had a good visit. He's an industrious boy. He told me all about his nephew and that you two are going to get to the bottom of this murder. I was intrigued."

"Don't be. We're not experts."

"But you've solved many-a-mystery, Gemini. Don't sell yourself short."

They pulled into the only underground parking garage in Charming. Gemini reached for the door handle, but Howard grabbed her arm. "During the peace treaty talks, I agreed to escort you to the door. That means helping you in and out of the vehicle. Sophia's rule, not mine."

After discovering her last outing, Sophia was furious. She called Howard to verify the facts and then let him know that if her mother was ever in his care again, he would have to follow her rules.

"If you must. Leo quit opening the door for me years ago, after we watched a documentary about feminism. He realized he'd been treating me as if I were made of glass."

Howard got out of the car and went around to the other side, holding out his hand. "Today, you are made of glass, my good woman. Think of yourself as an exquisite vase. If you break, we don't have insurance."

She rolled her eyes and bit her lip simultaneously. She still felt a little pain when she stood and sat, but she didn't want Howard thinking she was weak. "Does that line work on anyone?"

"Just you."

They found an empty bench in the park and Howard lowered her gently to a seated position. He stood by her side like a bodyguard, watching carefully as people walked by.

"Would it do any good if I told you how much I enjoy the outdoors and wooden seating? I mean, I'm not opposed to sitting in a park alone, but it would be a nice change of pace to hear what the boy has to say."

She was actually relieved that he was there, though she didn't tell him. "Stay. Maybe you'll have questions for Rigg I haven't thought of."

They watched as three boys and a girl chased each other around the colorful equipment.

"My Taurus needs more social time. He's going to grow up to be a strange young man if his parents don't let him do regular things like this." She gestured toward the children, who were in a pile on the ground now, giggling.

"Sophia requires a delicate touch." Howard rubbed his chin. "You may need to show her rather than tell her. Bring her to a park like this and she can watch how her son's anti-social tendencies cause him to feel awkward and left out. That should get her juices flowing. If she wants to create the next CEO, he'll need to be able to schmooze."

She stared at him, her mouth agape. "You certainly know more about Taurus than you let on. I don't think he's anti-social, but I'm not an expert at–"

"Mrs. Reed?"

They both looked up to see a young man who resembled a teenaged Tug. His eyes were a dark brown as well as his hair, and his skin was olive colored, but he was Tug in every other way.

"You must be Rigg. I've heard so much about you." Gemini attempted to stand and then thought better of it. "Have a seat. Howard Beachmont, my neighbor, will keep us on time."

Howard set the timer on his watch and nodded. "Nice to meet you, young man."

"Rigg Muehler. But you already knew that. Thanks for contacting my teacher. I wanted to talk to someone about what happened, but my family wants this to go away."

His sensitive nature reminded her so much of Tug. Telling him would only add more confusion to the boy's already turbulent world, so instead she admired a great family connection in silence.

"Rigg, can you tell us about Mr. Betz? Did you know him well?" Gemini asked.

Rigg placed his arm on the back of the bench behind Gemini. "My dad says he was a family friend from way back, but I didn't recognize him. He taught third grade and I'm a sophomore, so we didn't really interact."

He stared at Gemini's face with the same intensity as his uncle. "Are you going to find out who killed him? It seems really strange, even for my family, that nobody will talk about it. Part of me thinks they don't believe me about the way it went down."

Howard leaned forward, past Gemini. "We believe you, son. It's peculiar how they blamed it all on you though, isn't it?"

Rigg cleared his throat and began bouncing his knee up and down. "I'm kind of...weird. Everybody at that school thinks so. When I told the principal that I didn't have anything to do with Mr. Betz's death, she didn't believe me."

He ran his fingers through his thick, dark hair.

"My family is good at silencing people they don't like," he continued with a shaky voice. They ended the investigation, probably paid off the police. Now my dad wants me to go back to Smiley Academy. I told him everyone hated me before this happened and now it will be even worse. He didn't listen."

"You poor boy," Gemini remarked.

Rigg covered his face with his hands and began to sob quietly.

"It's all right, let it out, Rigg," Gemini soothed. She patted his back and a second later, he thrust himself into her arms.

She felt a twinge of discomfort but said nothing, instead hugging him as best she could. She looked over his shoulder at Howard, who was wearing a scowl. In her best attempt at thought transference, she tried to convey to him the importance of letting Rigg get it all out of his system. Gemini thought he'd gotten the hint when he nodded to her.

"In my experience, those who display the most emotion are the ones with something to hide."

"Howard!" Gemini scolded. "That's plain nonsense. This boy's been through a tremendous hardship. Please get Rigg a tissue from my purse."

He did as he was told, handing her a tissue. She pulled away from Rigg and handed it to him, running her fingers across his bangs to push them back into place.

"We understand how difficult this is, especially when everyone else in your life isn't taking it seriously. That's why Howard and I are here to speak with you. We'd like to hear your version of the events that happened that day."

Rigg wiped his eyes and sniffed. "It was lunchtime. I was sitting by myself, as usual. Someone said they'd heard my name over the loudspeaker, but they are always playing games with me. I ignored them, until I heard it myself."

"And what did the voice say?"

"First off, it wasn't the principal's voice, so that threw me. But it told me to come to the teacher's lounge kitchen. It's a separate room from the teacher's lounge. The kid behind me started snickering, so I figured they'd set me up again. Last month, one of them had me called to the track area. When I went outside, they took my key card and locked me out."

"You use keycards to get in and out?" Gemini asked, surprised. "That's an upgrade since Sophia attended. Please continue."

"I went to the teacher's lounge kitchen expecting something to be dumped on my head or someone to jump out and scare me. Instead, as I was about to go through the door, I heard arguing."

"Did you recognize the voices?"

Rigg shook his head. "It was a man and a woman. That's all I can tell you. I stood outside listening to them and trying to decide if I should go in and interrupt or just pretend like I didn't hear my name called."

"Could you make out what was said?"

"Just at the end. The yelling quieted down, and I heard 'Please!' and then, 'You had this coming.' There was kind of a gasp," he sucked in air, making sure Gemini was watching. "Then, silence. That's when I walked in and found him on the floor."

"You poor dear. That must've been so traumatic."

Rigg's eyes filled with tears once more. "It was. I've

never seen someone...you know...dead, before. He had a knife sticking in his chest and blood was coming out. I ran to the principal's office and told them."

"Rigg, the police did file a report and I reviewed it," Howard said matter-of-factly. "This is a sensitive issue, but what I read is that you had a bloody knife in your hand."

Rigg jumped up facing them both. "I didn't! I swear I didn't! When Dad brought me home, my hands were clean. And our lawyer said with the force it took to stab him, I would have been covered in blood, not just my hands. Someone set me up!"

Gemini put her hand in the air. "We believe you, dear." She wasn't so sure about Howard, but now was not the time to ask. "Can you think of anyone willing to kill to hurt you?"

Rigg gave her what she knew as the "side eye." Sophia always gave her the same look when she asked a question her impatient daughter found far too dumb to answer.

"You should probably start with the people who *do* like me. That's the short list."

Howard cleared his throat and clasped his hands together. "Son, I'm going to ask you a very mature question. I realize you're still a kid, but sometimes we have to be able to look at ourselves as others do."

"I know that."

"Okay, well...why do you think the other kids don't like you? Do you dress differently, or have funny habits?"

Rigg stared at the ground. "I know exactly why. But I'm not going to tell you. My Grandma Mitzi always says you can have difficulties, but if you share them with outsiders, they'll use them against you as your weakness."

Gemini and Howard were silent. Gemini knew Tug was close with his grandmother, Rigg's great-grandmother, despite Tug's disconnection from the family.

Howard's timer went off, startling them all back to reality. "Let's get you home, kiddo."

They all walked to Howard's car in silence. Gemini wanted to comfort him further, but she lacked the words.

"Rigg, I had a thought while we were talking. I'd like to meet with your great-grandmother. The women of the family always know all of the secrets and their origins. Maybe she can shed some light on this for us."

Rigg looked unsure. "Grandma Mitzi will be mad if she knows I talked to you. We're not supposed to share with outsiders."

"I'm not going to tell her we met today. I'm simply going to have a chat with her and see if she has any thoughts on Mr. Betz's murderer."

"If you think it will help." Rigg still appeared unconvinced.

"I've got her contact information, but you can help with this part. What would give her incentive to see me?"

Rigg smiled. "That's easy. Grandma loves charity work and homemade cookies."

When they reached his designated drop-off spot, Rigg paused before opening the door. "I want to thank you both for listening to me today. My dad and his lawyers never really asked. They just told me to keep my mouth shut."

Gemini handed him a tulip-covered business card, one she'd just recently received in the mail. *Gemini Reed, Conversationalist, Retiree, and Amateur Detective.*

"My number is on there. Call me if you ever want to talk again. Or I guess you kids prefer texting. You know, there is one other person who would receive you with open arms."

"Who?"

"Your Uncle Tug. I wrote his number on the back of the card."

Chapter Fourteen

FEATHER

"I feel as though we are kindred spirits, Feather. We don't always need words." Gemini squeezed her hand and kissed her forehead. "When you're ready for something more, you know where I am."

Gemini came to check on Feather, against Skye's wishes. Feather explained everything, even the painful experience with Tug in the emergency room. She stopped short of sharing more secrets of P.I.N.K. and Tag Junior with her though.

"When are you going to tell him about...Howard from the Iris Club?"

"I don't want to hurt him. It never feels like the right time."

"Take it from someone who has been in a relationship for several decades—secrets are the one thing that weaken your bond."

"Howard just texted that he needs to get you back," Tug said as he poured himself a juice.

111

She rose and waved as she left Feather's apartment.

"Thanks, Gem. I love you!" Feather called after her.

Propped on the couch under Tug's watchful eye, Feather was getting anxious about all the clients she'd missed. Some were very picky about their hairstyles and would have no qualms about telling her when she returned.

"Are we going to the gym today?" She asked, though she already knew the answer.

"Not until I'm sure you've got the energy."

"I really need to get back to the salon. We need new plumbing and there's a lawsuit coming up. None of those things will go away just because I'm not there."

Tug sat down and kissed the top of her head. "I know that, babe. Just give me two more days and I'll feel better about your returning to work. I've been keeping in touch with the staff, and everything is taken care of."

Feather's eyes widened. "That's what I'm afraid of. I love all the girls, but none of them are capable of management. And they fight about the dumbest things."

"You may be surprised. I've been talking with Stevie-the-new-girl and she has impressed me. She said she went to business school before she got her cosme-tology license. That girl has potential."

It was a little surprising that the mousy girl who had trouble asking clients to pay after she cut their hair was more than capable when it counted.

"She did take charge when I had the attack. I'm always underestimating people, it seems."

Tug, who was tucking her blankets firmly around her body, raised an eyebrow. "Why do I feel like that was a loaded statement?"

"I was just thinking about your ex-girlfriend, Julianne. You said you were close until your depression. Was there anything else that happened?"

Tug sat down beside her. "I'm just going to ask this once, and then I'll never ask again. Have you been talking to someone in my family? There's no other reason you would bring this up out of the blue."

Feather struggled for words. She didn't want to lie to him anymore, but knowing how much time she was spending with his brother would just kill him.

Soon.

"I didn't want you to be mad, babe."

He propped his knee on the couch beside her and crossed his arms over his chest.

"What? I thought we left everything on the emergency room floor, like the doctor suggested."

"I wasn't feeling well that day, so I didn't want to get into this, but now I'm doing better, so I want to be honest." She closed her eyes briefly, buying herself a little more time.

"The other day, one of your...high school friends... came into the salon."

"Which one?"

"I think he said his name was Brad? He said he'd

been thinking about you, and he wanted to meet me, to make sure I wasn't taking advantage of his friend."

Tug's face darkened and his body tensed. "He was such a jerk. No wonder he was asking about Julianne. He wanted to see how you'd react."

Feather thought about her time with Tag Junior. Even though he appeared earnest, everything he'd done so far was deceitful. He wanted her to tell Tug and upset him, she could see that now.

"He said to tell you hello." She looked down at her feet. "Yes, he was trying to upset me, I can see that now."

"Now everything makes sense. You were worried about my relationship with her because my old friend made it out to be much more serious than it actually was. Sounds just like him, always trying to pit people against each other. I hope he didn't make you feel bad. Just like my own family, everyone in his has a specialty. His is manipulation."

That's exactly what Tag Junior had been doing through their fake sessions together.

"I have no reason to speak to my family or Julianne's ever again." He made a chopping motion with one hand. "Future and past exist on two planes. The two will never meet."

* * *

Jayden Ko texted that they should meet before her next lesson with Tag Junior. When she arrived at the meeting hall, there was a sign on the door that read, "Mystics Seminar in session. Please enter through the laundromat."

As a child, she'd spent many hours playing with dolls on the broken tile floor while her mother did their laundry at the *Fold 'Em and Go* laundromat. It wasn't until Feather entered high school that her family bought their own washer and dryer. It felt like a huge luxury.

She paused as she entered the large room. Nothing had changed. The walls were still lined with bright, orange machines and the clock on the wall was still thirty minutes slow.

As she gazed at the pieces of her childhood, Feather completely missed the loose chunk of the commercial rug. She tripped and attempted to catch herself on a washing machine, but it was covered in a white, smooth substance that made gripping impossible. When her flight came to an abrupt landing, she found herself lying face first on a piece of tile missing one corner.

Cautiously, she sat up, feeling for anything broken or out of place. Another trip to Charming General Hospital was out of the question, especially since she'd received the bill from her last stay. Assured her body was intact, she reached to stand. That's when she noticed drops of blood on the floor and immediately put her hand to her mouth.

The last time she'd gone for dental work, the dentist's dead mother stood behind him, giving

Feather a complete rundown of his failings. She likened it to her own horror movie—listening to a person drilling on her teeth while another spoke of his incompetence.

Nothing was loose, thank goodness.

Reaching into her pocket for tissues, she noticed the hairs on her arm standing at attention. "Now?" she asked. "I'm in a crisis, can't you see that?"

Go to the mirror.

"The last thing I need right now is to see myself in the mirror!"

Exasperated, she tromped across the room, where a full-length mirror was attached to the wall. She moved in front of the mirror with hesitation. Her face was smeared with blood. Stepping in closer, she lifted her lip to find she'd cut the inside of her mouth.

"Okay, I appreciate the heads up."

Go to the mirror.

"I'm at the mirror! You may not remember this, but we humans have immediate needs. Right now, mine is finding some ice!"

It occurred to Feather that now was the opportune time to address this unwanted guest.

"I've been meaning to talk to you. I'm not sure why you're here, I'm sure it was a very painful experience. But maybe you could go outside? There is a lovely alley where you could find peace."

Go to the mirror.

She'd never found a spirit quite so obstinate. Maybe there was something more she was missing. She ran her fingers around the mirror frame for something out of place. All she found was a disgusting collection of dust.

"Nothing. I'm leaving now. I have a meeting. We'll talk again soon. The people here don't want you around. Think about the alley."

Mirror.

Feather huffed. "You may have a disability, and for that I'm sorry, but I'm done for to–"

Something caught her eye she hadn't seen before. There was a piece of paper slid in between the glass and the frame at the bottom. She'd completely missed it.

When she pulled it out, the paper was folded multiple times. Unfolding it like a small puzzle, the final result was a note smeared by humidity and dulled by the years. Feather was barely able to make out the words:

Tug,

I wanted to tell you in person, but your parents won't give permission for me to see you in the hospital. I hope you're improving, by the way.

Here goes nothing.

I'm being blackmailed. It's not that I don't deserve it, because I did something horrible. Unlike you, I don't have the strength for honesty, so I guess that makes me an easy mark. It's come to a point where I can't take it anymore, and discomfort is more important than truth in our world, right?

I'm going to turn myself in soon. Even though our boyfriend/girlfriend relationship didn't work out, you'll always be a part of my soul. Does that make sense? I'd do anything for you. Anything.

By the time you get out and read this, I'll be in prison. Please come see me. I'm scared.

Your loving friend,

J

She looked around the empty room and slipped the note in her pocket before continuing to the P.I.N.K. office. Wishing she had more time to ponder the note, she set her face in a pleasant smile before entering the office.

"I thought you'd forgotten. Just kidding. I know what happened."

Jayden, dressed in a leopard-print catsuit and cat ears, offered Feather a bottle of sparkling water and took one for herself.

"Sorry. I had an encounter with the spirit in the front. Oh, and do you have some–"

"Ice? You forget I'm an empath. I was preparing it before you arrived." She handed a plastic bag filled with crushed ice to Feather along with a cloth to wipe her face.

"You might have warned me. I don't need any more doctor visits," Feather grumbled.

"Sorry, I was on the phone when I heard of your arrival."

"If you knew I would fall, then you know about the conversation I just had."

Jayden ushered Feather into her office and sat down. "What do you mean?"

"You knew the message was about my boyfriend."

"No, I didn't." Jayden sat back in her chair, crossing her legs. "I have visions, but they aren't always complete."

Her demeanor was calm, too calm for Feather's liking.

"Before we talk about your encounter, I'd like to discuss Tag Muehler Junior. Go ahead and ice your face. I've got a lot to say."

Feather leaned back in the chair and placed the ice on her mouth, closing her eyes.

"It's come to my attention that Mr. Muehler may not be sincere in his efforts to hone his skills. Capu, wanting to keep communication lines open, invited him in for a private chat and Tag admitted he'd not learned anything from you."

Feather's head snapped upright, and the ice slid down her front. "What? I've sacrificed hours I could have used in my salon, and more importantly, with my boyfriend!"

"I'm agreeing with you. Please let me continue, and keep that ice on your face until I'm done."

Sheepishly, Feather tipped her head back once more.

"Yes, he claims you've not taught him anything. But when Capu asked him how he knew he was talking to spirits at all, he replied, they give him messages about things, not necessarily what he wants to hear. That's exactly what you should have taught him. He's learned that somewhere, and if it isn't from you, he's got another source for education." Jayden cleared her throat and continued. "Capu is eager to receive Mr. Muehler's donation, but at the same time, he's concerned about exactly what the man is trying to achieve. He wanted me to convey to you that your sessions will now be more of a fact-finding mission than an actual teaching experience. At least from our end. As far as Tag Junior knows, nothing has changed."

Jayden leaned forward. "I know how many demands you have on your time, and I told him just that. You don't have time for Mr. Muehler's games."

Feather nodded slightly, trying to keep the ice in place.

"That's when we came up with a plan. You and your friends have solved a great number of mysteries around town. We'd like all of you to investigate Tag Junior's family. We know Tug isn't close with them, which will make it a little easier on him. In exchange, we'll forgo the ghost in the laundromat issue for now. Most important to us is the knowledge that Tag Junior means no harm to the P.I.N.K. society. Think of yourself as a portal for good."

Chapter Fifteen

GEMINI

"I told my driver to pick me up in an hour. If that's too long, I can always text him." Mitzi Muehler sat her leather purse on Gemini's table and glanced around. "Cute place you have here. Is it your retirement home?"

Gemini brought a plate of orange frosted cookies, voted favorite cookie by the staff at Leo's care center, to the table and sat them down next to the frosted brownies and vanilla snappers. If Mitzi could be won over by baked goods, she was holding nothing back.

She returned with two cups of tea in mismatched mugs. There was no greater fete than her midnight cooking binge. Skye was sleeping in the basement, so Gemini snuck around like a mouse for hours, doing what she loved.

Today, Skye had an interview with her next patient and it couldn't have come at a better time.

"It's complicated. My husband is recovering from

an illness. Our plan was to live in Charming on a temporary basis, but we'll have to discuss it when he's better."

She sat down opposite Mitzi Muehler, wincing slightly, and trying not to make it obvious she wanted to study her features. Now that she'd met a third generation of the Muehler family, she wanted to see if she could spot a common trait.

Mitzi was a small, fragile-looking woman with a booming voice. Her energy matched Tug's.

"I have to tell you, Gemini, I've never been invited to tea before. We have business meetings and after-business dinners. My crowd doesn't do casual very well."

She took one of Gemini's orange cookies and took a small bite before placing it on the plate in front of her. "Oh my! These are wonderful! You'll have to give me the name of your bakery."

"No bakery. I make cookies every week and bring them to the salon where I volunteer. We call it the Friendship Room. It's a nice place to congregate and talk about our lives."

"In a salon? I've never heard of such a thing."

She didn't resemble either of her grandsons, that Gemini could tell. People always told Sophia that Taurus looked like his grandfather Leo. They both had strong jawlines but their demeanors were opposite.

"Do you like your neighbors? What's it like having them so close?" Mitzi took another cookie. "I hope you don't mind, I'm just curious."

"Not at all. I believe there's always something to be gained by talking to people outside of our normal circle. As to your question, it's not any different from the places I've lived before, space-wise. I have lovely neighbors who look out for me."

"My grandson tells me you were ill recently. I can see you have stitches and a wrap for your arm. Are you feeling better?"

"Much! Tomorrow is the last day with my insufferable nurse. I can't wait to be on my own." Gemini realized how much she enjoyed her routine.

"As nice as this is, I know you didn't invite me here for small talk. Let's get down to business." Mitzi brushed the crumbs from her face and sat up tall.

Even in her own home, Gemini felt intimidated.

"Well, first let me say, your grandson, Tug, is an exceptional young man. He's been a great friend to me and respectful and loving boyfriend to my dear friend, Feather."

Mitzi turned sharply. "Is that why I'm here? You want to convince me he should marry someone who isn't a part of our social circle?"

"No, that's not it at all." Gemini was taken aback. "There's been no talk of marriage, that I'm aware of anyway. And if there were, he couldn't find anyone more suited to him. But, as I mentioned on the phone, I'd like to talk to you about...The Ladies of Feather Works. We're a society of women who–"

Mitzi smacked her lips and set her cup down. "You can cut the nonsense right there, Gemini. You have to understand a woman of my means wouldn't arrive at a total stranger's residence without having them checked out fully first. I know of your considerable settlement with the hospital. If anything, I should be asking you for money!"

Gemini laughed uneasily. "Usually, I pretend like it's not there. I don't want it to change me, just pay my bills and take care of Leo's needs."

"So why did you invite me here then, if it wasn't to talk about my grandson's questionable life choices or a made-up charity? Or do you just like baking for random strangers?"

Gemini bit her lip before proceeding. "I asked you here today because I wanted to talk to you about your great-grandson. Rigg's recent experience is terribly upsetting. I used to be on the board of Smiley Academy, and we all want to find out what happened."

Mitzi's semi-pleasant expression changed to one of steel. "What do you know about that? Do you have a grandchild in that school? We paid handsomely to keep that out of the press. One of my grandsons even went to court to get the autopsy sealed."

"Would you like more tea?" Gemini stood, shocked to see the cookie plate empty.

"No, thank you. I'm very curious about your connection to this event. No one on the board has contacted me before today."

She sat back down, trying not to mull over Mitzi's characterization of the murder as an event, as if it were a concert.

"I'm an amateur sleuth. I've helped several people in the community when they've found themselves in a pickle. Your great-grandson swears he didn't kill Mr. Betz and I tend to believe him."

She paused to see what Mitzi's reaction would be.

With no inflection in her voice, she replied, "Go on, Gemini."

"I went to talk to Tag Junior about it and he didn't tell me much. I did get a glimpse of his wedding photo, though. I was surprised to see Diego Betz was a member of the wedding party. Do you know what his relationship was to your grandson and great-grandson?"

Mitzi drummed her pale peach nails on the side of her mug. "You're much more astute than the police. Not one of them asked about that relationship. There will be no investigation, by the way. The coroner has ruled it a suicide and the DA isn't pursuing charges." Mitzi smiled. "There are advantages to having money."

"Diego is, or rather, was the cousin of Martine. That was Tag Junior's wife. Horrid woman, horrid marriage. I've never been more relieved than when she removed herself from our lives, and especially Rigg's."

"Did you know Diego very well?"

Mitzi took another bite of her cookie and shook her head. "She didn't invite her family to the wedding, other than Diego. That suited us just fine. We knew the whole thing was a shakedown. She got pregnant to get her hooks into Tag Junior."

"And what of Rigg? Doesn't he ever ask about his mother?"

"He's a sweet boy. Never harmed a soul. I attribute that to my grandson. Tag Junior spent every spare minute with his son. He's as devoted a father as I've ever seen. The boy's mother, on the other hand, can't be bothered. Once she left, she never looked back." Mitzi sniffed.

"We used to buy elaborate gifts and have a staff member write loving birthday cards. We told him they came from his mother. When Rigg turned ten, he said, 'Grammie, those cards were written by your secretary. I recognize her handwriting. My mother didn't send any gifts either, did she?' "

"That must've been heartbreaking for you, Mitzi."

"She'll never know the damage she's done to that boy. And you know she ran off with my son, Chugg. I hope the two of them are making each other miserable."

Gemini hadn't expected Mitzi to be quite so open. By Tug's account, she didn't share with just anyone.

"Have you spoken with any of the school staff about the murder? In case they could offer some insight?"

Mitzi looked as though she might bite Gemini's head off and chew it alongside her cookie. "Why would I do such a thing? We've had it classified as a suicide and paid the staff handsomely to say so. My appearance at the school would suggest something different. I've never been there and don't have any plans to go in the future."

Gemini stared out the window, trying to think of a way to squeeze more information from this valuable source.

"Did Rigg know Diego was a part of his parents' wedding? Could it have upset him to have that man at his school, knowing his mother ran off and left him?"

"I don't think so. We've been very careful about the information we share with Rigg."

It was frustrating and heartbreaking to think of Rigg's world, tightly controlled by his family.

"You've got to remember, all those years ago we had to pull that wedding together in two weeks. Afterward, it was almost like it never happened."

"What? Why on earth? Martine sounds to me like a person who would want the perfect wedding!"

"Oh, she did. That's why it was so stressful. They dated for less than a month. We used to have family dinners on Sunday, and one Sunday evening, Tag says, "Grammie, I've got an announcement to make. Martine and I are getting married. She asked me and I said yes. You can imagine how loud it was when all of our jaws dropped to the floor at once."

Gemini thought back to Sophia's engagement to Brandon, well thought out and planned down to the date of the announcement. At least Brandon had that going for him. "I suppose there was no way to talk him out of it."

"We all pleaded with him, but he was adamant. He

brought Martine to dinner the following Sunday and she started making demands of us. She wanted her wedding to be this date and these many people. It was like we were her servants."

"Couldn't you have just told her no? That she and your grandson were on their own to plan and execute their wedding?"

Mitzi smiled once more, this time, it was more of a grimace. "You have to understand, when one of our family members marries, the entire business community expects an invitation. For them to run away and elope would have been a horrible slight to our partners. Martine knew that in advance, the devious little devil. When I suggested they wait a year, so that hopefully my grandson would come to his senses, she said, 'and have your first great-grandson insulted?' Well, I knew her game from that moment on. We planned the wedding for her and then waited for her to make her money grab."

"Let me guess, she tried and failed, so she went after your son."

"Gemini, you won't believe this." Mitzi leaned in close. "That woman tried blackmailing me. She said if I wanted to see my great-grandson after he was born, I would give her shares in our company. Of course I told her no. That's when she and Tag Junior met in secret with our attorneys. They drafted an airtight prenuptial agreement. When they reach fifteen years of marriage, Martine gets a sizeable payout and shares in the company. The devious little tramp," she huffed.

"To make matters worse, she set her sights on my son. Her revenge knew no bounds."

Mitzi's eyes brimmed with tears. "She zeroed in on the weakest link of the family. That's Chugg. I love all of my children, but he's that one member of the family that gives you indigestion."

Gemini thought about Sophia's husband, who caused her to lose her appetite more than once. "I understand completely."

"Poor boy stayed home the day they handed out common sense. I don't know when she started working her hooks into him, but she left Tag Junior and ran off with Chugg. We tried to secure a divorce for him, but she refused to sign papers and has tied things up in court for years. Her fifteen-year payout is this year. Makes me ill to think about it."

This wasn't an area Gemini wanted to touch. Chugg Muehler's faults were none of her business.

"Can you tell me anything more about her cousin Diego?"

"We really didn't know him well. I had my service check him out before he was allowed on the grounds, of course. He'd traveled the world building houses for the poor or some such thing." Mitzi made a sweeping motion, as if she had a fly in her face. "I never gave him a second thought after the wedding. One thing I can tell you for sure, if he was related to Martine, he had a deceptive streak. I wouldn't be surprised if another teacher found out about a scheme and killed him."

Chapter Sixteen

FEATHER

"That's it. Just close your eyes and listen. If you give them space, they'll talk," Feather said with a new lightness to her voice.

Now that the pressure of actually teaching him something was off, she felt less discomfort around Tag Muehler Junior. She was almost relaxed in his presence.

The ornate Charming Movie Parlour was a town icon and a tourist destination. When the Fire of 1924 came through, all that still stood on main street was this grand old lady. The locals took that as a sign of resilience and from that day forward, revered the building.

It was scheduled for demolition in 1957 to make way for a large department store, but the city hall overflowed with protestors until they reversed themselves and gave the theater its historic, thus protected, status.

Feather gazed around the space. The royal blue curtains framed a stage that had seen not only hundreds of movies, but also famous faces over its long life—including prestigious actress of stage and screen, Tulip Sloan.

She admired the large chandelier that hung above her head. When she was little, Feather assumed all movie theaters had them.

"Okay, I'm getting something." Tag gripped the blue velvet armrests tightly. "Yes...Gothburt says he has been here since the fire. Maybe that was the cause of his death." Tag opened his eyes. "Was there a death that wasn't reported? I thought everyone got to safety."

"Shh. Don't interrupt. Listen, remember?" Feather scolded. She hoped he didn't notice the smile creeping over her face. His performance was transparent and her enjoyment immense.

Tag leaned back against the headrest and closed his eyes again. "No, he was here in the nineteen forties. He remembers watching a newsreel before the movie that showed soldiers heading off to war. After that, he had his heart attack. He says he made up that first name."

Feather glanced at her watch. "We've been here two hours, so that's probably enough for today. How are you feeling? It can be exhausting until you've really got the process down. Ironically, these otherworldly beings tend to suck the life out of you if you let them." Feather laughed. "I never thought of it that way before, but it's funny."

Tag Junior laughed too, though his wasn't genuine. "You're a great gal, Feather. I have to say, my brother found the diamond in the rough."

Feather's brows knitted together with anger. "What does that mean? Are you referring to Julianne? Was she the first diamond he found?"

Tag tapped nervously on the seat in front of him. "Are they going to kick us out?"

She hadn't spoken to anyone about the note she'd found in the laundromat. Julianne had secrets she was keeping that Tag most likely knew nothing of. In time, Feather would investigate them.

"You have money. When we got here, you said it could buy anything, including time. I'm not worried."

"They loved each other very much. She came from a good home, her father was an investment banker, so we knew she wasn't after Tug's inheritance."

But you're worried about me.

"What changed?"

"My brother has been prone to fits of depression. He goes so low, there's no way to lift him back out of it. That happened when he graduated. He doesn't like change and the whole moving on theme didn't work for him. He wouldn't get out of bed for days. Julianne visited him a few times, but because of his weakness, she got bored and moved on. You can't really blame her."

Feather's chest tightened. "It's not a weakness at all. He's the strongest man I know both inside and out."

"We can debate that until the end of time, but all I know is she left for college, and he didn't. His excuse was some nonsense like, he didn't know who he was. He lost the best thing that ever happened to him. He broke her heart, and she never forgave him."

Tag Junior's version of events made his brother sound like a heartless man. It also didn't explain Julianne's note. The fact that he thought Julianne was the best thing to happen in Tug's life also stung in the center of her chest.

"You look like you have more to say," she said without any enthusiasm.

"No, after that, he had a series of, shall we say, less than desirable women? They were all after his money."

"And that's still what you think of me? An undesirable woman after his money? After all of our sessions together?"

Tag Junior displayed a smile that reminded her of the man who sold her a used car in need of thousands of dollars of repairs and bragged that she'd never find a better deal.

"I was just about to add that getting to know you has been a pleasant surprise. You're a much better person than I'd assumed."

She was fuming. There was no way to calm herself now, no matter how many breathing exercises she did.

"I've got to go. I have a cut and color in an hour. I'll see you again on Thursday."

She didn't wait for his response. Giving him the

satisfaction of knowing how deeply he hurt her wasn't in the cards today.

When Feather reached the safety of her car, she burst into tears. Out of relief to be away from Tag Junior or the story he told, she wasn't sure. None of his bitter words sounded like the Tug she knew.

She pulled down her visor and redid her makeup. Just as she was finishing, there was a knock on her window.

"Feather? Do you have time for a chat?" It was Jayden Ko, dressed in a blue and red catsuit with a watercolor theme.

"A short one. I've got an appointment soon. Why don't you hop in and we'll talk here?"

She unlocked the passenger door and Jayden slid in.

"How did you know where I..." Feather paused. Of course Jayden knew where she was. She was an empath.

Feather observed her exquisite makeup, which included hues of blue eye shadow and blue false eyelashes. "You're always the pinnacle of style, Jayden. If nothing else, this experience has taught me that I need to up my game. Someday, you'll have to give me some pointers."

"Oh, thanks." Jayden blushed and touched her blonde wig. "People never know how to take me. Some think I'm a joke and others think I'm proving a point. It's neither, actually. I finally became comfortable in the role of Jayden Ko. You don't need to up your game, you just need to make sure it's the right game for you."

The thickness of the air was gone, and Feather could finally breathe. Jayden was a safe space. "I just had a–"

"We need to talk about–"

Their voices intersected and they both laughed. "You go," Feather insisted.

"I forgot to ask you the other day when we met what you'd discovered from our spirit presence in the laundromat."

Feather felt heaviness again. Every conversation turned into a test. "Don't you know already? You told me you knew about my fall."

"I heard the message. The spirit guided you to a note that we never discussed. Do you have any idea where it came from?"

"The note? It was written by Tug's high school girlfriend. According to Tug, they grew apart. According to his brother, Tug was a jerk who drove her away." Feather put her elbow on the window. "The note leads me to believe Julianne–that's the girlfriend– had a big secret. When I have time, I'm going to do some research on her family."

"You don't sound enthusiastic."

"Well, Jayden, to be honest, I'm at my limit. I don't have any more energy, paranormal or otherwise, to devote to this right now."

"Feather, can I be frank?"

When people asked that question, it was normally used as a preface for nasty or negative words.

She steadied herself, preparing for the worst. "Go ahead."

"A decade ago, I made the decision to change my life. I became the person I was always meant to be. Before that, I worked for the F.B.I. as a profiler."

Feather gasped. "That's crazy! That wasn't at all what I expected you to say. I want to hear all of your stories."

"Another time, I promise. What I wanted to say is that I got pretty good at deciphering body language and characteristics of people who were hiding things about themselves, their personalities, or their actions."

"And you're going to tell me what you see in me."

"Your body is tight. Your fists are closed, and your shoulders are high. That's a sign of conflict. I'm sure you're overworked but combined with everything else on your mind, it's causing you great physical distress. Either take care of it, or it will take care of you."

"What do you mean?" She asked, though she was relieved Jayden understood.

"I mean, some of the turmoil you're experiencing can be fixed easily." Jayden placed her hand on the door handle. "Sit quietly and think about it. And while you're thinking, review our last conversation. It will bring you some clarity."

She opened the door and left as quickly as she'd arrived.

That night, Feather had the dream again. This time, she was running in a field of bright, purple flowers. When she was caught, the spirit encircled her body and threatened to cut off oxygen. It recited, over and over, *Turmoil threatens to explode the portal.*

Feather's eyes opened and she sat upright. "I understand now!"

Chapter Seventeen

GEMINI

Olive Thomas adjusted her panty hose and walked purposely into Smiley Academy. "I haven't dressed like a businesswoman since my husband's funeral. These shoes may be the death of me."

She'd borrowed Gemini's dress shoes, a pair of short-heeled black pumps.

"They're sturdy, Olive. They won't fail you." Gemini leaned back in the passenger seat of the van Tug borrowed. He was busily adjusting volumes as she spoke.

"Do you know what you're going to say?" He asked. "Give me a few more words so I can make sure we hear each other."

"Yes, I'm going to ask why my dear great-grandson was kicked out of Smiley Academy for a murder he didn't commit. And I'm not to embellish."

"That's the most important part," Gemini called. "Keep to the script, Olive."

"Okay, the target is in sight."

"It's not a..." Tug began. "Never mind."

"Hello, Mrs. Muehler? I'm Principal Wellstone. It's such a pleasure to meet you! We never had the opportunity to see each other while your great-grandson was a student. Such a tragedy!"

Gemini recognized the voice of the woman she'd convinced herself she liked. Now that she and Leo had been away for several months, she realized the woman's personality turned on a dime and she never saw a checkbook she didn't like. As judgmental and cruel as anyone she'd ever met, the only reason she treated Gemini with a morsel of respect was their mutual interest in the betterment of the school.

There was a sound of shuffling, and then, "Please wear this around your neck while you're here. We have a very strict policy about visitors."

"Yes, well. My poor little Rigg. He's beside himself. That's what I wanted to talk to you about today. And make a healthy donation, of course."

"Good for you, Olive. Those are the magic words," Gemini said under her breath.

"Of course. I'll be of help if I can."

"Can you just go over all of that again? I'm an old lady and my memory isn't what it used to be. What happened that day?"

Principal Wellstone sighed. "Well, according to my staff, your great-grandson left the lunchroom in the middle of his assigned lunch break. We've had some issues with Rigg, I'm sorry to say."

"Rigg?" Gemini was surprised to hear his principal describing the gentle boy as a troublemaker.

"Oh, sure," Olive replied. "Kids get upset so easily these days, don't they?"

"Some kids do. We don't know why he chose Mr. Betz, but a child prone to anger can lash out at anyone they deem an easy target. He took a steak knife from the teacher's lounge and lunged at the poor man. It was just awful."

"Rigg never entered the room," Gemini commented. "And he told Howard and me that he wasn't even in the teacher's lounge until after Diego was stabbed."

"And this is what my grandson admitted?" Olive continued.

"No, a staff member forgot some paperwork and came back to retrieve it. That's when she found Rigg standing over the body. Of course, we called the authorities immediately."

"Poor Rigg. That horrid Mrs. Wellstone is trying to frame him. If the police won't do anything, she'll make sure his name is ruined," Gemini whispered.

"My grandson is adamant he didn't kill anyone. He said he was called to the lounge over the loudspeaker and then found Mr. Betz dead. Like a Shakespearean tragedy if they had steak knives back then."

Gemini and Tug exchanged eye rolls over Olive's ad-lib.

"Well, you know how kids can make up stories. I'm sure he was in shock, as we all would be. He may not even remember the actual death. That's how we protect ourselves, you know. We block the memories out. I can assure you, this staff member is the most respected instructor here. She knows what she saw."

"Is there anyone else who might have had a key card to enter the building?" Olive asked.

"We only give them out to parents of students. Because you had an appointment today, I was able to have a guest card waiting for you. But no, there are no other guest cards that were issued on that date."

"Ask her if you can go into his dorm room and pick up the rest of his things," Tug instructed.

"I was wondering if I might go into his room and collect the rest of his things. If he goes away to the big house, we want mementos."

"Not good, Olive," Tug said tersely.

"You know, I have a nephew who went to prison. He's going to be in there for the rest of his life."

"No! Olive, no!" Gemini hollered.

"He and his girlfriend cooked up a scheme to make money on some new drug. If you ask me, it was the girlfriend's idea. My nephew was a good boy until he got tangled with that one!"

"Olive, stick to the script. You're almost done."

"Now that you've explained your family situation, I can see more clearly why Rigg might have reacted the way he did."

Gemini's blood boiled. "She's so condescending. I

should have pulled Sophia out of that school. There isn't one redeeming quality about it!"

"What?" Olive was caught off-guard. "No, you don't understand. He's from the other side of the family. The two of them aren't related. My great-grandson's a good boy. He's not going to prison. He didn't do anything. You know, his father is fixing things so he can come back next semester."

"Yes, we've been so appreciative of your generous donations. I can arrange for his things to be brought to my office tomorrow. I'm afraid I can't allow you to go to the boy's room. There are privacy issues, and his roommate is distraught. We don't want him to feel victimized too."

"Ask about the funeral," Tug urged.

"I'd like to pay my respects for your Mr. Betz. Can you tell me when they're having his funeral? I've been keeping an eye out, but there's nothing in the papers. I'm glad there's nothing about my grandson, but I thought at least I'd find an obituary."

The principal cleared her throat. "We pride ourselves on our discretion here at Smiley Academy. We know the right people to keep things private. As to the funeral service, it's my understanding that the family decided to forgo one. They don't want it to turn into a media circus."

"Good job, Olive. You're done."

"Well, I reckon I can come back tomorrow and pick up Rigg's things. You know, I'm still trying to wrap my head around all of this. Would you mind showing me where this happened?"

"Olive! Get out of there before you stumble!" Gemini called anxiously. She turned to Tug with concern. "Now that she's off-script, anything could happen."

"I suppose there wouldn't be any harm in showing you. The police have finished their investigation."

The sound of chairs moving and standing caused Tug to pull his headphones off and turn the mic down.

"Maybe she should ask about the coverup?" He looked at Gemini.

She hated being so blunt with Tug, knowing it would hurt him. "Your family paid her off, Tug. That's the coverup."

"Do you know the policeman who came? I've got a neighbor who is a retired police captain. As handsome as they come."

Her shoes clunked as she walked. Each time she tripped, both Gemini and Tug held their breaths until they heard the rhythm of her feet again.

"No, not personally. I'm sure they treated him well. We had a student last year who damaged the locker rooms, and they were kind to him. Here we are."

"Oh my. That's it? Never been at a murder scene before. Do they always smell so lemon-y fresh?"

"Our cleaning staff spent several hours scrubbing it down. They didn't want any trace of the event.

Everyone needs to move on as quickly as possible, so that we don't have a repeat offense."

"Do you think it's going to happen again? My Rigg isn't here."

"No, but students tend to copy each other. Someone else might decide that's how they get out of a bad grade. That sort of thing."

"Olive, it's time to go. You don't want to overstay your welcome," Tug warned. "You've done a great job."

"Well, Mrs. Wellstone, I need to get home to my knitting circle. Those women are all about finding dirt on my great-grandson. I thought I'd check with you first to make sure one of them doesn't surprise me. It sounds like everything is being handled."

"About the check..."

"Oh, right."

They could hear Olive fumbling with her purse.

"I brought cash. People of my stature don't like messing with checks. It's so middle class, don't you think? You can count it if you want. Twenty-thousand, it's all there."

"Olive!" Gemini cried.

"Thank you for your donation, Mrs. Muehler. I hope your great-grandson gets the help he needs."

Her shoes clomped a few steps and then stopped.

"Well, isn't that something."

"What is it, Mrs. Muehler?"

"Oh, nothing. I just noticed this spot where the poor teacher died, there are knife marks all over the side of the counter. Do you s'pose my grandson was planning to carve him into bits?"

"Olive! No!" Tug and Gemini said in unison.

"I...I'm not sure why that is. I'm sure your grandson didn't do that. It's probably some student who was fooling around with cutlery."

"Does that happen often? Your cutlery is used for games?"

"Mrs. Muehler, I'm afraid I've run out of time for today. I'll escort you back to the front door and you can pick up your grandson's things tomorrow morning. I'm so very sorry things ended this way for your family. Having two members entangled in the legal system is a burden I wouldn't wish on anyone."

Two sets of heels clacked until the sound of another door opening. Gemini and Tug watched as Olive made her way clumsily down the steps.

"I hope she doesn't break an ankle," Gemini remarked.

When she reached the far end of the parking lot, where the van was parked, Tug opened the sliding door and helped her inside.

"Well, that was enlightening. That's one fancy school."

Tug handed her a Tug Bar and a cup of water. "You did a great job! Can you tell us about the murder scene?"

"It's been wiped clean. And there is no evidence that a teacher was lost. That school is like a creepy horror movie."

Chapter Eighteen

FEATHER

Feather's sleep, as short as it was, turned out to be the most productive night of the year. She got up and wrote down exactly what she'd learned.

Jayden said to take care of the portal. I am the portal she was talking about. If I don't take care of myself, I will fall apart. Starting today, I'm coming up with a plan to change my life for the better. I'm going to get rid of some of this stress.

When Tug appeared four hours later, rubbing his eyes, he paused in the doorway.

"Are you really up at this hour? Every time I suggest going for a run at sunrise you tell me it's illegal."

She stood and kissed him on the cheek. "I figured it out. Not all of it, but one of the messages I've been getting. *Turmoil threatens to explode the portal.* I'm the portal, Tug. The spirit was warning me that I need to make changes in my life."

"Isn't that what we decided when you were taken to the emergency room? What's changed?"

She took his hands and spun him around. "Everything, my dear. I've spent the night making plans to change my life and yours."

Tug sat down at the table and looked at her worriedly. "I hope that doesn't mean you're kicking me to the curb. I was just getting used to your middle-of-the-night burps."

"No, silly. I decided I'm going to put the salon up for sale."

"What? Feath, you love that place! Why would you do that?"

"I love my work. I don't love dealing with the drama between stylists or leaky pipes. I want to cut hair and go home at the end of the day and do other things, like talk to ghosts."

Tug studied her face. "Okay, I guess that makes sense."

Feather went to the refrigerator and removed a bottle of green juice. She shook it well and poured it into a glass before setting it in front of him.

"Your Tug Juice is so much better with cucumber. I'm glad you made that change."

He took a big swig and set the glass on the table. "Don't keep me in suspense. You didn't spend four hours making one decision."

"I'm going to use the money from the sale of my salon to buy a warehouse."

Tug grinned. "What are we warehousing?"

"It's not 'we', it's you. This will be the factory location for Tug Bars. Since the salon was a gift, I don't
owe any money on it. That means the entire amount
from the sale will go into buying a nice big place. We
can get a loan for industrial baking equipment so you
can start distributing them outside of Charming."

Tug stared at her, blinking rapidly.

He reached for her and she moved to his lap, wrap-
ping her arms around his neck. His voice cracked as he
said, "Feath, that's the kindest thing anyone has ever
done for me. But I can't let you spend your money on
me. You should use it to open a proper paranormal
detective agency."

"I'll do that in the front of the building. We'll
section it off so I can have an office. I won't need much
space. I've been scouring the internet for buildings,
and..."

Tug squeezed her so hard she lost her breath.

"Feather Jones, you are one of a kind. No one ever
believed in me the way you do. You're my soulmate."

She felt shame because at that moment, she wasn't
thinking about Tug or his business. She was thinking
of Julianne's note.

"I feel the same way about you, Tug," she said
softly.

"I know I promised never to ask you about this
again, but I have one more question about Julianne.
Did she have people in her life who made her uncomfortable? Someone she wanted to escape from?"

Tug frowned and loosened his grip.

"Why the continuing interest in her? I haven't thought about Julianne since her death, and lately it seems like it's all that's on your mind. This is our day to celebrate the future, Feath, not hash over the past."

"Oh, I had another vision last night. A spirit was telling me...was telling me...that Julianne had unfinished business."

Tug scratched his chin and looked down at the table. "Okay, if we're going to talk about this now, I might as well get it all out in the open."

She sat down beside him. "Partners in business, partners in life. I won't judge you."

"As I told you before, Julianne was my high school girlfriend. Before twelfth grade, she'd attended a private school on the east coast, so she really didn't know many people. She liked to keep her friends separate from me. Her excuse was, 'Oh, they'll fall for you, Tug. You can't meet them.' "

Tug's imitation of a woman's voice was high and squeaky. Feather couldn't help it, she let out a hearty chuckle.

"Sorry. You're so cute when you're doing a horrid impression. Please continue."

"Yeah, so after we'd been dating six months or so, she says, 'Tug, I have to tell you something. There's someone from my old school who won't leave me alone. I don't know what to do.' "

"What was the friend bothering her about?" Feather asked.

"She was pretty vague. She said something about a

hazing incident, but that she couldn't tell me any more. I was a high school kid, and it didn't occur to me to ask about it again. She never brought it up after that time." He looked up at her with love in his eyes. "Now, can we please put this to bed? Whoever was bugging her is long gone. It's just you and me now."

"Thanks for telling me. You're right. It's over." She stood and leaned over the table, kissing him passionately. "And now, let's get on with the future! Get dressed, we're going to look at warehouses!"

Chapter Nineteen

GEMINI

"I don't believe we're going to solve this case without some help. Now that we're all investigating the Muehlers together, I feel pressure to get this right." Gemini placed her feet on the overturned bucket Howard generously offered. "I could really get used to this treatment. Watch out, I may be losing organs more often," she chided.

"It's a pleasure to wait on you. I don't have visitors often, as you know. I like that you and I can talk without worrying about what the other one says. That in and of itself is worthy of a few perks."

Gemini took a drink of her iced tea and leaned back in her chair, enjoying the warm sunshine. "Oh, Howard. You've really outdone yourself. Infusing your garden blackberries with mint really makes a unique flavor. I'd like to take some home. I need a celebratory drink now that my prison matron has moved on."

"One of my best mixtures yet." Howard smacked

his lips. "Where did you say Nightmare Nurse was going?"

"She was very secretive, just another family in need of her skills. I wonder if they know that resume includes a stint as a torturer?"

Howard chuckled. "Your Sophia missed the mark on this one." He took another long drink and set his tea on the ornately embellished metal chair. "I made teabags just for you. They're in the kitchen. Now, about your dilemma..."

"Yes, about that. I can't get over the idea that I'm missing something here. Diego Betz was Martine's cousin, but I can't find any other connections to the Muehler family. Rigg never met him before attending the Smiley Academy, so he would have no reason to be angry with him either."

Howard rubbed his scruffy chin. "Do you think everyone is being honest with you?"

"While she was delightful, I don't entirely trust Tug's grandmother. She has a huge chip on her shoulder. If it is truly because Martine hurt the family, it makes sense."

"But..."

"But if I were guessing, I would say killing Diego wouldn't be the way to get revenge on Martine."

"You did mention it had been a number of years since Martine was ensnared with this branch of the family. Has she been in contact since Mr. Betz's death?"

Gemini shook her head. "Not that I'm aware of.

Not with most Muehlers, including her son. She's been with Chugg Muehler ever since leaving her husband. When I contacted his office to reach her, I was told she's a fragile flower, unable to function. Not their words, but mine."

After Skye left for parts unknown, Gemini sat at the computer, trying to find any family information for Diego Betz. Even the private files for board members' eyes only didn't list a next of kin.

"I looked for a memorial service location, but just like at the school, there is no evidence he died. No funeral, no service, nothing. Just like Olive said, it's like nothing ever happened at Smiley Academy."

"Why don't you contact the funeral home and see who is responsible for arrangements? If they need you to go in person, I'd be glad to drive you."

It was getting embarrassing and humiliating that Gemini wasn't allowed to drive herself anywhere yet. In what now seemed like a deal with the devil, she signed a "contract" with Sophia and Skye that she wouldn't make this leap to independence until they both gave the okay. It was somewhat miraculous that Skye would scurry off to her next job without taking the car keys with her.

"You have things to do, Howard. It's unfair to keep involving you in my activities."

Howard raised his brow. "I'm surprised at you, Gemini Reed. You should know by now that there is very little in my life that won't survive a change in timeline."

"Well, if you're sure..." A smile crept across her face.

"Positive."

They were almost giddy as they drove into the parking lot.

"You know your story, Howard?" Gemini asked.

"Watch my thespian skills, Gemini Reed. You'll be putting my name in for the next award's show."

Chapter Twenty

GEMINI

"What was it you wanted?" The funeral director, a serious-looking young woman with copper-colored hair, asked.

"If you don't mind my saying, your hair is such a beautiful, unusual color," Gemini gushed.

She studied the woman's name tag, which read, "Lauren Carter, caring for your loved ones since 2010."

"It's a family trait," she replied somewhat sharply, taking Gemini aback.

"My husband and I..." Gemini looked at Howard uncomfortably, "are concerned that we weren't contacted about our nephew's services." She wasn't against making up stories, but this felt like cheating on Leo, even though it was just a means to an end.

"And what was his name?"

"Diego. Diego Betz."

Her demeanor immediately changed. "Oh, you

should've said so from the beginning. This was the most unusual afterlife care we've experienced."

Gemini felt a tickle in her nose. She wasn't expecting the funeral home to smell like a flower shop. She was fine with outdoor plants, but inside, too many flowers made her sneeze. She still tensed when she was ready to sneeze or cough, expecting pain in her abdomen.

"In what way?" Howard leaned forward, placing his forearm on the desk in front of him. "If it's a matter of discretion, I have no trouble making a contribution to whichever fund you deem important."

Gemini gazed at him with admiration. Howard always found the right words. She felt a tickle again and opened her purse in search of a tissue.

"I...uh," Lauren's eyes darted back and forth. "Okay, they must've told you about that. I'm not comfortable taking any more money from your family. Your nephew has already been buried in a private ceremony. Just his mother in attendance. This was our first experience in illegal activities, so you can understand our discomfort."

"Of course, dear," Gemini said, comfortingly. "We've heard many stories, and we want to make sure we aren't basing our decisions on rumor. If you'd relay to us all you know, we won't tell anyone it came from you and I promise, we won't bother you again."

Howard nodded in agreement. "My wife and I want to understand the circumstances of our nephew's death. My wife hasn't slept a wink since we heard." He nudged Gemini slightly.

"It's not healthy for a woman of my age to go long without sleep," she added. "I'd like to withhold myself from your services as long as possible."

Now she really did feel a sneeze coming on. Not just a polite sneeze, but the kind that produced an unwelcome chirp.

Lauren slapped her hands down on the desk. "Here goes nothing. Your nephew was brought in with a gunshot wound to the chest. There was also a steak knife sticking out of his chest, but it was definitely stuck in him post-mortem. He wasn't taken to the hospital, the ambulance brought him to me. When the EMTs arrived, they shook their heads, letting me know not to ask questions. A man soon followed. He offered me a very large sum of money to keep Mr. Betz's death and interment quiet. It wasn't optional, the man who came here had a gun."

"Do you think–"

"That he was the killer? That crossed my mind. That's why I didn't call the police after he left. He made threats against my family. I just couldn't take the chance."

"We understand. Was there any indication that Diego struggled? Any bruising?"

"Yes, now that you mention it. He had bruises on his arms, as if someone was fighting with him and trying to push him away. Small, circular bruises."

"How odd. Wasn't he found in the teacher's lounge, dear?" Howard asked.

"Yes, I believe he was. Excuse me, I need to tend to my needs." She stood abruptly, causing Howard to frown.

"I'll be back in a minute, dear," she reassured him.

Gemini stood in the hallway, where she could still listen to the conversation while allowing the allergy situation to happen.

Lauren leaned over the table. "That's the other thing this man mentioned. He said there was a confrontation and Mr. Betz died accidentally while on the playground. I'm no fool. That wasn't an accident."

He was dead when I came into the room, Mrs. Reed. I saw him lying in a pool of blood.

"Who was this man? What name did he give you?" Gemini called from the hallway. She blew her nose hard and was dismayed to realize she may have to use the very last tissue in her possession, the one of questionable origin at the bottom of her purse.

"He wouldn't say. He was an older gentleman, probably around your age, sir." Lauren gestured toward Howard. "He had lots of hair, dyed black and big bushy eyebrows. Not at all friendly."

"Did he make the arrangements?"

Lauren nodded. "I was told not to publicize the graveside service and that if anyone besides his mother attended, I was to turn them away. He said he'd be watching."

"One more question," Howard said in a low voice.

"How long do you think he was dead before he was found?"

"My guess," Lauren whispered, "is that he had been there about two hours. Rigor mortis had set in. After all the secrecy surrounding his death, my curiosity got the better of me. I found an online chat room where they were discussing his death. They said it was a student who found him."

"We heard that too. It's a shame, isn't it? A child shouldn't be subjected to adult games. Our family is struggling. Did you find out anything else from this web page?"

"No. That was enough for me. I figured the less I knew, the better." Lauren took a deep breath.

"I'd love to show you and your wife some options for your own passing. If you take care of everything now, you won't have to place your arrangements in the hands of unscrupulous family members..."

Gemini took the opportunity to meander around the mortuary. There were five viewing rooms and one marked, "Private." Satisfying herself that the "we" Lauren had mentioned was just an "I" Gemini opened the door quietly.

It was a small office containing a tidy, white desk with a single pink carnation in a vase on top. She moved in further, examining the books on the shelves.

"Unpestered Passing, Eulogies for Dummies, Rules for Funeral Etiquette," she read. "My, they'll publish anything these days, won't they?" Gemini commented.

Out of curiosity, she removed Eulogies for Dummies and began thumbing through.

"Use a flattering picture. If your last memory of your loved one is a homely picture, your eulogy will reflect that."

She chuckled out loud.

"I'm not sure where my wife went..."

Gemini shoved the book back on the shelf quickly. As she did, something fell to the ground. It was a yellow paper, most likely a receipt. She placed it in her pocket and closed the door.

Thankfully, Howard and Lauren were still sitting in the office. Howard's booming voice was only used to warn Gemini they were coming out soon.

"Sorry about that. I never know when these attacks are coming. What did I miss?" She didn't bother sitting down. She could tell by the pitch of Howard's voice that he was anxious to leave.

"Lauren was telling me that she thinks it was a mafia situation. She's seen enough movies to know them when she sees them." Howard waited for Gemini to look in his direction and then rolled his eyes.

"You never know, sweetums, we have some very dark corners on our family tree," Gemini replied dryly.

"In all the movies I've seen, even though they kill their loved one, they make sure they have a nice burial. They are the mortician's dream," Lauren added without emotion. "Without knowing any more, I'd say that's what happened to your nephew. I'm sorry. I'm sure you're both grieving. But you can always..."

Howard stood. "We'll think about that After Death Honeymoon Package and get back to you. Matching coffins are hard to resist."

After they were seated in Howard's car, he turned to Gemini.

"I know you were snooping while I heard about all fifteen funeral packages Lauren sells."

"You know me well, Howard. " Gemini pulled the yellow paper out of her pocket and unfolded it.

"It's a receipt."

She studied the words, hardly believing them.

Chapter Twenty-One

FEATHER

Feather crossed off the last warehouse for sale in the Charming area. "You never know, that place might come down in price."

They'd found the perfect location for their joint venture—1818 Flying High Lane. It had ample space for Tug's factory floor and kitchen. There was even a brightly-lit, sky-blue office area for Feather's paranormal investigative business. The only problem was that the price was twice the value of the salon.

"I know you're disappointed, but we're going to find the right space for us, Feath. It's just a matter of time." Tug patted her leg as they drove up to Forty Cups for lunch.

"It was like a boulder had been lifted off my back when we decided to do this together. I'm feeling let down." She sighed. "Lunch with my best guy will make it better though."

They sat in a booth next to the window. Feather

watched the cars, mostly tourists this time of year, driving down the street as she sipped on her orange soda.

"Now that I understand at least one message from my dreams, I want to find a way to simplify every corner of my life. Even after a trip to the emergency room, it took me some time to realize the changes I need to make are drastic."

"It's nice that we'll all be working together, Feath. I don't mind investigating my family, but I wish you'd tell me why. I wouldn't put anything past them. And you know that Gemini, Olive, and I are working on the mysterious death of Diego Betz. You always say everything happens for a reason. There has to be a connection between the two, right?"

The expression on his face was the same one he displayed when he told Feather he'd surpassed his dead-lift goal.

Feather nodded eagerly. "Gemini must love the idea of all of us working together. She always says we're kindred spirits."

"My, I sound intelligent when other people are using my words."

They looked up to see Gemini, resplendent in a blush-colored top and tan pants with matching lipstick.

"Gem!" Feather jumped up and kissed her friend on the cheek. "What are you doing here? Did you drive yourself?"

"No, Howard dropped me off on his way to the

gardening center. I find I do some of my best thinking over a piece of Genevieve's marionberry pie."

She slid in beside Feather and moved the silverware setting in front of her.

"I'll go get the server," Tug offered.

"No need, Tug. They know my standing order." Gemini grinned, always grateful for his friendship and care.

"Now, let's get down to business. What I heard was that we are combining our investigations. If that's the case, I need to show you both something."

She opened her purse and pulled out the yellow receipt she'd found at the funeral home. She unfolded it and set it in the middle of the table, so they could all view it.

"I was doing some snooping in the mortuary that took care of Diego Betz. Lauren––that's the mortician, told us she'd been paid to look the other way about Diego's death. This receipt says otherwise."

Feather examined the receipt. "It says Muehler Holdings." She looked up at her friend. "I don't get it."

"Muehler Industries is the family company. Muehler Holdings is the company set up by my Uncle Chugg," Tug explained.

"Why would she write out a receipt for illegal activities?" Feather asked. "That doesn't make sense."

"It does if you know Uncle Chugg. He's always looking for a way to make a buck. That means writing off everything from his weekly pedicure to the house he built with Martine. He should have been a sleazy accountant instead of just a run-of-the-mill sleaze."

"I was puzzled too, Feather." Gemini replied. "Then I remembered that Lauren said he wanted everything kept quiet. Chugg came in and paid for Diego's funeral, most likely to keep his death quiet. Martine, if she really is as fragile as I've been told, may not even know about her cousin's death. I suspect Lauren kept a copy of the receipt to blackmail Chugg later on."

Gemini's dark-purple berry pie, slathered in ice cream, arrived alongside a steaming mug of coffee.

"Thanks, Bertha. Tell Genevieve I'll be bugging her for the pie recipe."

"All fingers point toward Chugg, then," Tug replied grimly. "He's not an upstanding person, but what would his motive be? He's already got everything he wants from our family."

Gemini took a bite of her pie and wiped the melting ice cream from her lips. "When I met with your grandmother, she mentioned that Martine was about to receive a sizable amount of money from her prenuptial agreement. Maybe Chugg is trying to make sure there's no one else to cut him out of his share."

Tug sighed happily. "Look at us. We're our own little family of investigators. We each have our own super power. I realized that every time we solve a mystery, we do it as a foursome."

"Oh, Tug, about your nephew——Howard arranged for another meeting tomorrow with him. It's his weekly Tae Kwon Do lesson and we wanted to ask him a few more questions. Would you like to come?"

"I want to come too! Maybe he's got a spirit near him who will tell me more!" Feather said excitedly. "I have a color and perm, but I think we'll be finished by two-thirty. She doesn't have much hair."

Tug's happy expression became sullen.

"I see your wheels turning. What's going on in there?" Gemini asked Tug with concern.

"I've missed out on most of his life. What if he hates me?"

The bell over the door jingled and Olive appeared. She waved at the threesome and bounced with excitement to their booth.

"I went to the salon early for my appointment and they told me you were gone. Tug forgot he left that tracer on your car and the app on my phone." She waved her bedazzled phone in the air proudly.

"This week's driver, Tedrick, was none too happy to drive me clear out here to the edge of town, but I thought it was important to discuss my color before my appointment. I'm a little hurt you three are having a party without me."

"Cheese and crackers, Olive! If we'd known we were having a planning meeting, you would've been the first person we'd call." Gemini scooted over and patted the bench. "Take a load off."

She slid in and stared at their somber faces. "Oh boy. It must be bad! All I wanted was to talk about my color. I'm thinking I want some pink stripes, just like you have, Feather. Can you make them so bright that Phyllis Peterman gets a headache?"

She picked up a fork and began eating Gemini's pie. "Haven't had marionberry in years."

"Is that the lady you were telling me about while we were making Choc-O-Rama Tug Bars, Olive? The one who complains about everyone and everything?" Tug asked earnestly.

Olive nodded and crossed her arms over her sweatshirt with the words, "Fancy Pants" embroidered across the chest. "Nobody likes her. She tried to steal Brenda's seat at dinner. You know we all have our favorite places to sit. Well, when we told her that was Brenda's place, she wrinkles up her face and says," Olive squished her nose and placed her hands on either side of her eyes, "I must sit here or the last of the daylight will give me a splitting headache."

"I've had clients with light sensitivity. It's a real thing, Olive." Feather was growing antsy. This discussion would start over once she had Olive in her salon chair.

Olive pushed her hand forward. "No, that's not it, I assure you. The woman complains about everything. If someone wears jeans she says, 'That fabric gives me a headache. Take them off.' That kind of thing."

"You remember how difficult it was for you when you moved in? Maybe she's feeling the same way," Tug suggested. "It's always hard to be the new person."

"I don't know about that. She thinks she's the queen of Charming Retirement Center. But enough of my troubles. Tell me what's what at this meeting of the minds."

"We're making plans for tomorrow, Olive. The three of us will meet Rigg at the park."

Observing Olive's dejected look, Feather added, "and you will catalog all of our findings so far. We need to look at all of the evidence together, right everybody?"

Chapter Twenty-Two

FEATHER

"I don't think he's coming," Tug said, pivoting to return to his car.

Feather grabbed his arm and planted herself in place. It wasn't an easy task given his titan-level strength. "He's only five minutes late. Just be patient, I know he'll be here. Gemini promised and she isn't someone who breaks promises."

They watched as mothers and children walked by, the children excitedly relaying stories of their school day.

Feather recognized him as soon as she saw him two blocks away. He had the same gait as his father and his uncle, and the beginnings of a muscular build. His face was different, probably resembling his mother more than his father.

Gemini put her arm around him and they strode in unison to the picnic bench. She was always trying to make people feel comfortable, Feather mused.

As they drew closer, Rigg's eyes diverted to the ground in front of him.

"Rigg, this is your Uncle Tug, the guy I've been telling you about. He can help you with your weightlifting questions. Do you know, he won a regional contest once? He was Mr. Charming," Gemini said matter-of-factly.

Rigg's head snapped up. "Really? That's the most competitive contest on the coast! That's cool!"

Tug's tight posture relaxed, and he stuck out his hand. "I did. Twice, as a matter of fact. It's nice meeting you, Rigg. I haven't seen you since you were a baby."

Rigg shook Tug's hand and returned his eyes to the sidewalk in front of him.

"I'm Feather Jones. I'm your uncle's girlfriend." Feather held out her hand. As he shook it, she felt a zap of electricity. He averted his gaze quickly.

"Nice to meet you."

"There's a picnic table over here where we set out some snacks. Should we all sit down and talk?" Gemini asked.

She'd set out energy drinks, junk food and lots of Tug Bars. She wanted to make sure she'd covered all corners of the teen palate.

Rigg sat down across from his uncle and picked up a Tug Bar. His eyes widened. "You have your own protein bar? That's so cool!"

"Try one. Let me know what you think. We haven't even tapped the teen market yet. These are all sample flavors." He scooted the Chocolate Dream and Olive's Orange Oolala over to the other side of the table and Rigg immediately tore one open.

"I'm sorry for what you went through at that school, buddy. It must've been real scary," Tug said.

Rigg's eating slowed momentarily. "He was a nice guy, at least that's what everyone said."

"I'm sure the police asked you all of these questions already–" Tug began.

"No, they didn't. My dad told the police not to ask me anything, so they didn't."

The three adults exchanged glances.

"We wanted to bring Tug up to speed. We're all doing our best to find out what happened. That's what you want, right?" Gemini asked.

He reached for another bar, his third, and ripped the wrapper open. "These are great, Uncle Tug. I'm taking some with me, if that's okay?"

Tug grinned. "I've never heard myself called, 'uncle' before. I have to say, I love it. Take as many as you want."

Rigg filled his coat pockets with as many as he could and tore open another Chocolate Dream.

"You must've been so confused," Feather said abruptly.

The adults all looked at her with surprise.

"You could say that," Rigg replied casually.

"Anyway, if you can think of something else, something we might have forgotten to ask, you can–" Tug began.

"I mean, hearing a murder must've really confused you. Didn't you tell my friend, Gemini, that you heard voices in the room?"

"Feath, what are you doing?" Tug whispered. "He's just a kid. Don't grill him!"

"Trust me!" she replied tersely.

"I dunno. I guess. Yeah, I did tell her that. I forgot."

Gemini touched Feather's shoulder, trying to get her attention, but for the first time in their relationship, Feather shrugged her off.

Rigg sighed. "I told this story already. I waited until the voices were done yelling, and when it was quiet, I got up and went into the room. That's when I found him."

"Mr. Betz lying on the floor?" Tug asked. "Terrible."

Rigg nodded solemnly. "With a steak knife in his chest. We just started first aid, so I didn't know what to do. I ran out and found a teacher and told them. That was it. I was told to go up to my dorm room and not to talk to anyone. Pretty soon, my dad came and took me home."

"Rigg, what did you hear when they were yelling?" Feather asked. "This is important, think hard."

Rigg looked at the table, where only one Chocolate Dream Tug Bar remained. "I can't remember. Just a bunch of yelling. Maybe saying stop or something." He took the last bar and tore off the wrapper.

Gemini retrieved a small notebook from her purse

and licked her fingers as she perused the pages. "Here it is. Rigg heard, 'Please!' and then, 'You had this coming.' There was kind of a gasp." She closed the notebook and glanced at Rigg, whose face was beet red, and then at Feather, who was clearly upset by her helpfulness.

"Do you think they were talking to each other, or to you?" Feather persisted.

He looked at her with disdain. "Why would they be yelling at me? They didn't know I was there!"

"Diego and his murderer didn't know you were there, but someone else did. Think, Rigg!"

"Feath, the kid doesn't know!" Tug snapped. "Why don't you tell me about all the sporting activities you do? I'd love to hear..."

"The voices you were hearing weren't from the teacher's lunchroom, Rigg. They were in your head," Feather said quietly.

Rigg laughed uncomfortably. "You think I'm crazy? Wow, that's even worse than my family."

"I don't think you're crazy. I think you have a gift. The voices you heard were spirits warning you. They were yelling at you, trying to keep you from entering the room."

Rigg frowned as he digested that information. "I don't know why you'd think I'm some kind of a–"

"You're a medium. That means you hear voices of those who've passed. Sometimes, they come to warn us. That's what the spirits were doing for you, Rigg. They didn't want you to get hurt."

Rigg stood. "Thanks for the bars, Uncle Tug. Your girlfriend is crazy though. I gotta get home."

"Rigg, wait!" Tug tried grabbing his arm as he galloped away from the group.

"Let him go, Tug," Feather cautioned. "He needs time to think."

"You know how badly I wanted this, Feath," Tug said, his eyes brimming with tears. "Why would you upset him like that?"

Feather rubbed his arm. "He needs to understand his gift. The more he knows about it, the safer he'll be. Believe me, I don't want to jeopardize your relationship, but he needs to understand what happened. It's for his own safety."

"I certainly understand now why he doesn't want to return to Smiley Academy. He mentioned the other day that he's an outcast and now it all makes sense," Gemini commented. "Poor boy. Adolescence is hard enough without dealing with something like this."

It was all starting to make sense. Tag Junior's pretend gifts weren't his at all, they were Rigg's.

Chapter Twenty-Three

GEMINI

"Did you tell her our exciting news, Tug?"

Gemini glanced at Tug and Olive with surprise. "What news? What am I missing?"

"Well, I got a call from the new gift shop two blocks from the salon. They want to carry my bars!"

Gemini took his hands and jumped up and down, forgetting for a moment about her tender parts. "That's great news," she replied, grabbing her side.

"Not so fast," Olive cautioned. "We've gotta make two hundred bars in three weeks. We're up to our gills in bar samples as it is. Where are we going to put everything?"

"When we're done with this case, I'd be happy to help you find a place. For now, you're welcome to use my kitchen. It's not much bigger, but the stove is brand new."

She'd been thinking about something for a long

time now, but it didn't seem appropriate to tell them. Not yet.

"You're sure recovering fast, Gemini Reed. I need to know your secret. Can't hardly see your stitches anymore, and you've just got that wrap on your arm. It's like it never happened," Olive remarked with awe. "Some days I wonder if you're really as old as you say you are."

"I've heard of women pretending to be younger, but never older, Olive. But thank you. My daughter sent me some overpriced products to use on my scars. To my chagrin, they work very well."

It's called Scaraway Serum, Mother. It's two hundred dollars an ounce, so don't spill it like you do your cheap makeup.

Olive put her hands on her ample hips, her *Tug Bars Official Assistant* apron hanging loosely around her neck.

"Now that I'm closer, I can see that you look a little peaked, today, Gemini. Tug, why don't you help her to the couch?"

Instead of waiting for him, she shoved Tug aside and assisted an unreceptive Gemini to the couch.

"I'm really fine, Olive," she protested, even though she did feel slightly tired.

The scents of cinnamon and chocolate enveloped her as soon as she sat down and she realized she hadn't eaten all of the lunch Skye made.

"What are you making today, Olive? It smells wonderful!"

"Today we're trying another new one. We're calling it, Cinna-mania. That was Tug's idea." She smiled appreciatively at Tug. "I've got a batch I just finished glazing. I'll bring you samples."

Gemini returned her attention to Tug. "Interesting turn of events, your nephew with the gift."

Tug sat beside her and put his hands on his knees. "It is, isn't it? In our family, it would be considered a burden, not a gift. Anything that makes him less mainstream will unfortunately be the poor kid's undoing."

"Howard and I were talking about it on the way over, and I think the next move for me is to contact Rigg's mother. If she doesn't know your Uncle Chugg is dangerous, I need to tell her."

"How are you going to get a message to her? That place is a fortress."

"Never underestimate me, or Howard. We have endless resources. In the meantime, I don't believe I've asked about your relationship with Diego Betz. What do you remember of him?"

"Not a lot. It was a long time ago." Tug thought for a moment. "All of the groomsmen with the exception of me and my cousin, Jagg, were college buddies. Tag Junior thought of them as his true brothers." Tug rolled his eyes.

"Okay, here you go, Ms. Gemini."

Olive set a plate of warm bars in front of her, alongside a cup of tea. "We haven't had our control group test these yet, so you're the first guinea pig."

Olive took a piece and brought it to Gemini's lips. "Down the hatch," she insisted.

Gemini pulled her head away, tired of being mothered by Skye. "If you'll set it down, I'll eat it."

Olive, oblivious to Gemini's distress, shrugged her shoulders and popped the bite into her own mouth.

"Olive, I think I smell that the next batch is done. You know how tricky our oven temperature can be." Tug grinned as they both waited for her to disappear into the kitchen.

"Sorry, Gem. You know Olive, she gets excited about things. She means no harm."

"I know. I'm overly sensitive since my two weeks with Nightmare Nurse." Gemini placed one more bite into her mouth. "These are all wonderful, Tug. I don't know how you'll decide on your final four."

"Thanks, Gem. We're thinking of having a contest. We'll put samples out at the salon and ask people to vote."

"Any nibbles on that yet? Feather told me about her plans to sell."

"A few of the beauticians have expressed interest, but nothing firm."

Gemini took another bite and chewed it slowly, savoring all of the flavors.

"Back to Martine, I'm worried you'll get hurt trying to reach her. Uncle Chugg is a paranoid man and believes in lots of security. It wouldn't surprise me if he's already caught wind of your suspicions and locked his place down."

"That's why I came here first. I'd like you to give me a little more information about Martine, so I don't have to waste time with small talk."

Tug stood and put his hands in the pockets of his gym shorts. "Our family likes to hide our imperfections. Martine is one of those. She and Tag Junior got married against the wishes of my grandmother. She was sure she was after the family money."

With Olive safely out of the room, Gemini took a bite of the last sample Tug Bar on the plate, called Raspberry Razzmatazz. "Oh, Tug! This is a winner!"

"You really think so? Your opinion means the world to me!"

"I do. Just personal preference, I'm sure."

"When Rigg was a little over a year old, Martine started acting funny. She'd stay out late with friends, sometimes not returning until the next morning. She lost interest in Rigg and Tag Junior. This is all according to my grandmother, since she's the only one besides Rigg who still talks to me."

Gemini's heart ached for Tug. "You're such a fine young man. If your family would open the door just a crack, they'd be amazed by the person you've become."

Tug smiled warmly. "Thanks, Gem. Not everyone is as forgiving as you. They look at my rejection of the family business as a personal rejection. That's why Martine's betrayal was especially hard. She cheated on my brother and then I turned down my place in the family business. That's when they really closed ranks."

"I don't know how to ask this delicately, but what about–"

"The affair? In true Muehler fashion, it was never spoken of. I mean, like the next day we pretended like Tag Junior had been raising his son on his own all along. Chugg is her son and even though he isn't part of the family business anymore, Grandma still speaks to him, like she does to me." Tug rubbed the back of his neck. "For the two of them to carry on like that, it's unforgivable. It must hurt Rigg."

"When I spoke with your grandmother, she didn't mention a word about him."

"That's why I think it's impossible you'll be able to see Martine. I'm sorry, Gem. You're always so resource-ful, but this time, I don't think you'll be successful."

"Successful at what?"

They turned around to see Feather standing in the doorway, her hair ruffled and her eyes blurry.

Tug kissed her on the cheek and smoothed her hair back into place. "How was your nap, babe? Do you feel better?"

She nodded. "The nightmares really mess with my sleep and naps don't leave me with time for anything else. If this doesn't resolve soon, I'm going to lose my mind."

"We're so worried about you, dear." Gemini patted the couch beside her, and Feather came and sat down.

"Your family—Tug, Olive, and I—are here to support you. Tell us what you need?"

Feather smiled and laid her head on Gemini's

shoulder. "I know. You guys are wonderful. This is something I have to figure out for myself though. What's going on with the investigation?"

"We were just discussing that, babe. Gemini wants to speak with Martine."

"There is one more thing, Feather. I'd like you to come with me to visit Tag Junior again and see if you get any messages from spirits. He's a funny sort, but you never know who or what might be in the room."

Feather's face turned ashen. "I...can't do that."

Tug rubbed her shoulders and kissed her neck. "We understand. You're so stressed right now with your own problems. Maybe down the road--"

"Not down the road, not ever!" Feather snapped.

Olive came into the living room and all three of them looked at Feather with surprise. It wasn't like her to snap at anyone, let alone those closest to her.

"No need, dear. We'll find another way." Gemini rose from the couch and handed Tug her teacup and plate. "Delightful, as usual, Tug. I'll be in touch. Love you both!"

You're looking in the wrong direction.

She glanced around the café, where the only other patron was drinking a coffee and reading the morning paper.

"What's here? What should we be doing?" Tug asked excitedly. He had become so in sync with her actions that he could tell when she was talking to a spirit.

"They are telling me to look in the other direction. I don't know what that means."

Tug stood and took in the room.

"Tug, sit down, please. Let's not be obvious," Feather pleaded. "It could mean anything."

"I'm going to the restroom. On the way back, I'll take a stroll by the outer tables and see if anything is out of place."

There was no arguing with him when he was this focused. If it made him feel connected to the spirit, it wasn't a bad thing. "Okay. But don't make a scene."

"What, me?" he asked in mock offense.

When he left the table, she closed her eyes, imagining herself sitting on the beach with an umbrella in her drink. *Let's talk. I'm ready to listen.*

She pulled out an imaginary book of hairstyles and began reading. The tap on her shoulder was light, but she knew it was the soul she was waiting for.

"I won't look at you if you don't want me to. What is it you're trying to tell me?"

You're looking in the wrong direction. The sun is over there.

Feather shaded her eyes, gazing out over the ocean. "No, it isn't, the sun is behind us."

A long arm appeared beside her, pointing toward the horizon. Over the smooth surface, a tear formed, and the ocean ripped to reveal a spinning ball.

Look in the other direction.

"I don't know what you mean. Unless...yes!"

"Feath? You having another vision?" Tug shook her shoulder.

"Yes, sort of. It keeps telling me to look in the other direction, but there is no other direction. Sometimes they talk in code and really frustrate me. Did you find anything on your trip to the restroom?" She hoped he didn't sense the sarcasm in her voice.

"There is a picture on the wall between the restrooms. I think you should see it."

Feather got up to follow him, but he disappeared.

That was the moment she realized she was dreaming again.

"Tug?" she panicked. "Where are you?"

You're looking in the wrong direction.

She felt her head being pushed in the opposite direction, where broken tiles covered the floor.

Feather sat up in bed, sweat running down her back.

"Tug!" she called. "Where are you? Are you safe?"

The door to their bedroom slammed open and he ran to her side. "What's going on? Another bad dream?"

She nodded, trying to catch her breath. "I didn't know where you were or if you were even alive."

He brought her into his chest and held her tightly. "I'm not going anywhere. I promise."

She pulled away and glanced at his worried face.

"I've been looking for a solution to the laundromat ghost problem, and there's something that's always bothered me."

"Yes?"

"Why is this particular spirit haunting the laundromat? It was an empty lot before the building was built. There must've been a death at the *Fold 'Em and Go*, Tug. Not a peaceful one, something this entity wants me to uncover."

Chapter Twenty-Five

GEMINI

"Are you sure you're up for this, Gemini? From an amateur's standpoint, it seems you're rushing into life headlong. I thought you were instructed to take things slowly?"

Howard shut off his car and turned to look at Gemini.

Mrs. Reed, your level of activity is against my wishes. I promised your daughter I would check in every week and clearly you're not following my directives. That's a real bug-a-boo of mine. Even if you are no longer my patient, your lack of recovery would reflect badly on me. I'm not above informing your son-in-law.

"I'm quite ready, Howard. I need to speak with Rigg's mother and find out why she abandoned him. I won't sleep at night until I do."

"This time, I'm going in with you. I won't take no for an answer. This is a potentially dangerous situation and you're still in recovery."

She opened her mouth to protest, but once Howard set his mind to something, it was impossible to change it.

They approached a massive adobe structure with floor-to-ceiling windows. Gemini pushed the doorbell, and an automated voice answered. "Please enter the code given to you by the occupants. If no code is entered within thirty seconds, security will escort you off the property."

Gemini pulled the rumpled paper from her purse quickly and entered the numbers. "I didn't have time to pull out my readers, so security may be coming for us, Howard. Did you bring your self-defense weapons?" she mused.

A lovely trio of bells rang, and a staff member opened the door. "Mrs. Reed and guest, we've been expecting you." He ushered them into a sunken living room area with a long couch lined up around the outside. "Please be seated. Your host will be here soon."

"Not the friendliest fellow, is he?" Gemini sat down and placed her purse beside her and looked around the empty space. "Minimalist is what I think they call this. Boring is what I call it."

Howard rubbed his hands on his thighs. "Something about this bothers me," he whispered.

"Mrs. Reed?"

They both stood, surprised to see a man sporting fluorescent orange glasses frames and a lime-paisley pajama set. His hair was wild and curly, his eyebrows and mustache following suit.

"I'm Chugg Muehler." He thrust his hand forward.

Gemini was the first to take it, shaking firmly to meet his equally firm grip. "I thought we'd made an appointment with Martine Muehler?"

"She's been detained. And you are?" He turned to Howard.

"Howard Beachmont. Pleasure to meet you, Mr. Muehler."

"Only members of my family call me that. I'm Chugg to friends, Choo Choo to closer friends, and Chugster to my Squeaky. That's my nickname for Martine."

After introductions, they all sat on the couch with Chugg seated across the room on another section of the same couch. His large stomach was barely contained within his bright green flowered shirt.

"Martine says you wanted to discuss her son. It's a sensitive topic for her."

"I can certainly understand. After so many years, she's probably unable to bring herself to make contact."

Chugg opened his mouth. Instead of a gasp, a high-pitched giggle came out, surprising all three of them. "Oh, aren't you the cutest thing? Can I call you Gemini? I love that name, by the way!"

Somewhat flustered by his reaction, she nodded. "What surprised you about that statement."

"You haven't heard the whole story. Martine and I fell in love before she married Taggy. We met at a family dinner early in their courtship and hit it off."

"Your mother thinks she set her sights on him right away. Why didn't the two of you stay together?"

Chugg looked up at the ceiling, where three giant ceiling fans moved rhythmically. "I'm much older than her. She thought, and rightfully so, that our families would fight us. She told Tag Junior right away that she wasn't in love with him. He blackmailed her into marrying him anyway."

"What was his bargaining chip?" Howard asked.

"Martine, my dear, my world, had a bit of a spending problem. She took his credit cards and ran up a debt, to the tune of eighteen thousand dollars. That was just in the first month after he gave them to her."

"She could've promised to pay it back in install-ments," Gemini protested. "She didn't have to marry him."

Chugg giggled once more. "Precious, that's not how things work in the Muehler family. If you've tarnished the Muehler name in any way, you'll be punished for the rest of your days." He squirmed until his body was upright. "Let me tell you a story."

"Excuse me, Mr. Muehler? Did you or your guests want anything to drink?"

A maid entered the room so quietly no one noticed. She rocked back and forth on her toes and pursed her lips.

"Not now, Jess. But thank you. Unless you need something?"

Both Howard and Gemini shook their heads, and the maid left the room.

"Now, where was I?" Chugg put one short, chubby leg over the other and sat back. "My spoiled brother, Tag Senior, used to bring home strays, as Mother called them. They were pretty young women with no pedigree. Mitzi raked them over the coals so badly that by the time dinner concluded, they escorted themselves out. No amount of money was worth her harassment. That's when he gave in and married the woman his parents chose for him. A loveless marriage, but one that made everyone happy. Tag Senior swore his sons wouldn't be subjected to the same protocol, but old habits die hard, especially in our family. Wouldn't you know it, Tag Junior brought home strays too. One day, he brought the woman who was to become his wife."

"If she married him, she must've handled the mother-in-law pretty well," Howard commented.

"Au contraire." Chugg stuck one finger in the air and shook it. "She was treated the worst of all of them. The difference was, at the end of the evening, she got in Mother's face and told her in no uncertain terms that she was a future member of the family. That's when I knew she was the love of my life."

"What happened then?" Gemini was getting impatient. She wasn't sure if her pain medication was wearing off, or if his flippant attitude was the problem.

"She got pregnant." Chugg sighed. "Mother found out about the baby and the credit card debit the same day. It didn't go over well. Martine was forced to marry Tag Junior in order to pay off her debt."

"To a man she didn't love," Howard reiterated.

"But she had a nice prenuptial agreement drawn up. I have some experience in the field of law, and I know that takes forethought," Gemini insisted.

Chugg's face lost all of its color.

"How do you know about that? Oh wait, don't tell me. It was Mother, wasn't it? That's been sticking in her gullet all of these years. Martine's father wanted to protect her, that was all. He knew how ruthless my family can be. It was wise, don't you think?"

"What happened next?" Gemini asked.

"The marriage was an unhappy one," Chugg continued. "She gave birth to Rigg and found herself excluded from his care. Mother made sure Martine was otherwise engaged when it came time for his feedings or baths, or even playtime. We were still communicating in secret, you understand. I helped her leave, of course. We planned for months. Tag Junior's always been a sound sleeper, so Martine would sit in their massive closet and we'd talk all night. We planned her escape for the night of the Charming Ball, the biggest social event on the coast." He paused.

"I don't mean to be insulting if you've gone before. I'm assuming you haven't. Lovely pair, you two. I just don't see you as gown and tux kind of folks."

"I've been twice. Never had a decent meal nor conversation," Howard grumbled. "Please finish your story."

"Everyone was concerned about Tug's mental health, so they hired security to watch over him. When Martine faked a headache to stay home, no one gave it a second thought. I arranged for Martine's belongings to be delivered to my home and she walked out the front door. Mother, to no one's surprise, was furious. She thought Martine planned it from the first day of their marriage. I assure you, my sweet little Squeaky never did such a thing."

"That's very sad," Gemini commented without waiting for Chugg's reply. "She never bonded with her son?"

Chugg shook his head emphatically. "Not in the least. We planned the whole thing together, when to leave, what she could take. Then she looked at her son and realized the Muehler family would hound her forever, as long as she kept their heir. She made the painful decision to leave him." Chugg wiped his brow with a bright orange cloth from his pocket. "We've been together ever since, fourteen years now."

There was much to gain from this conversation, but Gemini needed to stay focused for now.

"Poor Martine. Has she tried seeing the boy while he was at boarding school? You know her cousin worked at the school Rigg was attending, right?"

"We have our spies." Chugg's eyes darted back and forth. "Yes, we knew he was there. Martine lost contact with her own family when she married into this mess. They weren't interested in supporting her connections and she wasn't ready to fight for them, so she gave them up. We were sorry to learn of Diego's passing. We were planning to attend the funeral, and then Martine fell ill."

"Chugg, I know a little something about how big corporations work," Howard began. "There are always moments when someone can sneak away for a private message or call. It can be done."

"She could, I suppose. But it was one more fight, and frankly, my little Squeaky had no more fight in her."

"When might we speak with her?" Gemini leaned forward, trying to find a comfortable position to sit.

"Not today, I'm afraid. She's a bit of a frail, wilted flower. When she heard her son was responsible for her cousin's murder, she took to her bed. She hasn't been up since."

"That's sad, and of course we do understand." Gemini thought for a moment. "Do you suppose you could take a note to her?"

Chugg's face lit up. "A note? How very nineteen-ninety of you!"

Gemini dug her nails into her knee. "Or whatever you think might be the best way to contact her. I've been investigating the murder for your nephew, Tug. He believes Rigg is innocent."

He stared at her with skepticism. "That poor boy. Tug was far too loving and sincere to fit into our family. He would believe the boy was innocent. He's been away from the family too long, I fear. He has no idea what they're capable of. Even young Rigg."

Howard folded his hands in front of him. "Tug is a man of excellent character. You may be surprised to learn he's done just fine without the family."

"Hmm," Chugg responded dismissively. "Tell you what, when Squeaky wakes up, I'll approach her cautiously and see if she would be up for a little drive to meet you. The fresh air will do her good. Would that be all right?"

"Yes, fine." Gemini stood, looking at Howard expectantly.

"Oh, it is time for us to go," he said, receiving her message loud and clear. "We'll look forward to hearing from you, Mr. Muehler."

"Wait!" Gemini yelled, startling both men. "I need to use your restroom. You get to a certain age and there's always some kind of plumbing issue."

"I can show you–" Chugg began.

"I'd rather your maid show me the way. I'm a little old-fashioned when it comes to these things."

Chugg pushed a button on the coffee table and his maid appeared momentarily.

"Please escort this little diamond to the closest guest bathroom. Make sure she doesn't stumble."

Gemini growled softly at his inference that she was somehow feeble, but said nothing. When she returned, it was obvious both men were relieved to see her.

"Chugg was just telling me that his mother stayed in contact with Diego. He wanted her to invest in some kind of drinking water project in Zimbabwe."

She tried not to act as shocked as she felt.

"Your mother and Diego? She never mentioned a word."

Chugg raised an eyebrow. "Mother usually isn't open with strangers."

"She was feeling lonely that day. I was just thinking how odd it would have been for her to stay in touch with one of Martine's relatives." Gemini's face was crimson, and she turned to face the window so it wasn't noticeable.

"Well, it's time for my afternoon siesta," Howard announced. They said their goodbyes and walked out to the car, both keenly aware of Chugg's eyes following them.

"When we got there, you said something didn't feel right. Were you able to decipher exactly what that was?" Gemini asked as she pulled her seatbelt across her lap.

Howard shrugged. "I'm torn. There was guilt all over his face, so I know he's hiding something. I looked at the furnishings in the living room and noticed that nothing came from Muehler-owned companies. I do know my furnishings, and I can tell you, it was all imported. I guess that's not a big deal though."

"I agree, Howard. But more importantly, he is keeping Martine from seeing us. A mother protecting her son goes to any length to prove his innocence. On the way to the restroom, the maid explained that Martine was taking a new medication that made her drowsy. She didn't seem to realize we came to see Martine today."

"Now that you mention it, that's odd. Why do you suppose Mitzi Muehler was in contact with Diego

Betz? Do you think she felt threatened by him? Keep your friends close and your enemies closer, that sort of thing?"

Pushing the visor down, she touched the corners of her mouth to ensure her lipstick was still in place. "I also want to point out, he was a large man with very bushy eyebrows. The same description our friendly mortician, Lauren, used."

"By jove, you're right!" Howard slapped his leg. "What's our next step, my amateur detective friend?"

"I gave the maid a note to pass along to Martine. I asked if we could meet without Chugg."

Chapter Twenty-Six

FEATHER

She was running on an endless racetrack. There was snow falling on her head and it smelled like something familiar, something comforting, but she couldn't quite make out what it was.

Turmoil threatens the portal.

She was out of breath and paused, placing her hands on her knees. A dark presence overtook her, creeping up the front of her body until it reached her throat. Just as it was about to take her voice, she grabbed the hand and held it firmly.

"I understand that I'm the portal. I'm working on that issue. I figured out the second riddle too. What else do you want me to do?"

The entity whispered, "Look in the mirror." She glanced at a mirror in front of her, where her image was turning in circles. In a few moments, the glass shattered.

Feather bolted upright, breathing heavily.

"What is it, babe?" Tug asked sleepily, reaching over to comfort her. "Another bad dream?"

She threw the covers off. "It's nothing. Go back to sleep." Walking over to the mirror, Feather realized she was terrified of what might be there waiting. Something gruesome or bloody, maybe the image of a spirit rotted in the ground?

She turned on the bathroom light and allowed her eyes to adjust to its brightness before stepping in front of the mirror. There was just a girl who lived a hard life, who fought through every challenge, who didn't know who the enemy was this time.

Maybe it wasn't this dark spirit in her dreams she was afraid of, maybe it was her own soul.

Letting that percolate, she pulled a brush out of her drawer and began brushing her wild, pink hair until it was all in place. She stopped abruptly when it came to her.

"Tug!" she called. "Oh, never mind."

She turned on the light on his side of the bed and gently rubbed his shoulder. "Babe, if you're already awake, I'd like to talk."

Tug rolled over and patted Feather's leg with one hand while rubbing his eyes with the other. "I'm up."

"The messages in my dreams are telling me to care for myself. I'm the portal and I need to eliminate some of the stress in my life if I'm to continue. But the spirit wants me to dig deeper."

Tug stared straight ahead.

"Tug? Did you hear me?"

He nodded. "I did. Let's sleep on this and talk about it more tomorrow." He yawned and rolled over, pulling the covers up to his chin.

Feather remained seated. She poked him in the ribs. "Tug?"

"Mmhm..."

"There is one more thing I've been wanting to ask you about. It's probably one of the reasons I'm still not sleeping."

"Okay, shoot." His muffled voice replied.

"Your high school girlfriend, Julianne. How did she die?" She still hadn't shown him the note she'd retrieved from the mirror at the *Fold 'Em and Go*.

Tug rolled over and pushed himself into a seated position. "Feath, you're starting to sound like a broken record. We talked about it the other day and I explained everything I knew."

"I can't shake the idea that she is connected to all of this. I need you to start from the beginning and tell me everything."

Tug sighed. "This is the last thing I want to discuss tonight."

"I know. But if it will help me sleep..."

"You already know about our relationship and how it ended. And then, she died. What else is there?"

"Your brother seemed to think–"

"What?"

An awkward silence filled the room.

"Now I'm fully alert. What do you know about my brothers? Is that why you've been asking all these questions about Julianne? Did somebody contact you?"

She was at a crossroads. If she told him the truth now, there would be more questions. She wanted to wait until she had all of the answers.

"No, it was a spirit. He was somebody's brother, that's for sure. Just not yours."

Tug didn't look convinced. "If it is really one of my brothers, they'd already decided I wasn't worth the Muehler family name because I wasn't committing to a university sport like the last four generations. Any information you get from my family is suspect."

"That's why I'm asking you, Tug. I don't trust him —the spirit—not one bit."

"And secondly, I was in a deep depression before Julianne left. Sure, I was upset she was going away, but she didn't cause my depression. We'd already broken up, and if you want me to be honest, I think she was dating someone at the university. Now, can we please go back to sleep?"

She leaned over his body and kissed his face. "Her loss is my gain."

"But you're searching for something more, right babe?"

"There was someone who tried to blackmail her. Did you know that? Did they ever try and contact you after Julianne's death?"

"Why would they? We weren't together."

"Just wondering. You get some sleep now."

"You're not going to bed with me? I'm awake now

and I could use a snuggle!" Tug protested, patting the bed beside him.

"Soon, my love. I need to write out my thoughts while I drink a nice cup of tea. I'm starting to sound just like Gemini."

Chapter Twenty-Seven

GEMINI

"That's when we left, Leo. You wouldn't believe that house. The paint was questionable though. I'm sure they hired a substandard company."

Today they sat on the patio of Charming Acres Assisted Living Care Center watching the hummingbirds flutter above the buttercup yellow daffodils. It always made her feel better, knowing she could tell Leo about her activities.

Leo, positioned upright in his wheelchair, was able to grip a cup of water for short periods of time. His speech was still nonexistent, but it didn't matter. He was alive and moving.

She took a bite of Tug's latest bar creation, the Black-and-White Tug, a mixture of white and dark chocolate with nuts. "Oh, you've got to try this, Leo. It's the best one yet." She broke off a small corner and placed it on Leo's tongue. His mouth moved slowly, unable to master completely the task at hand.

It reminded her of feeding Sophia when she was little. They would place tiny bits of lemons, pepper, and tomatoes on her tongue to give her the experience of trying something different. It wasn't important that she eat, just that she had the idea of food. Leo was experiencing tastes and textures as a toddler would.

Gemini took her napkin and captured what fell out of his mouth.

"Leo, let me tell you, this one really has me stumped." Gemini shaded her eyes and watched as a woman and her nurse walked through the garden area. It was almost as impressive as Howard's, with a multitude of colors and shapes making a glorious display. She would have to mention it to him. He was always interested in what others did with their gardens.

"Chugg Muehler is a strange bird and my number one suspect. His only motivation for killing Diego would be keeping Martine away from the rest of the family, but it seems they already cut her out."

She squeezed his hand as she did every day. She was certain the time would come when he would squeeze back.

"And then there is Mitzi Muehler. She didn't even mention she was in contact with Diego Betz. That's odd, don't you think? And Rigg Muehler's father, maybe he was upset by his son's treatment at the school, but it doesn't explain setting up his son to look like a murderer."

She held Leo's hand firmly and watched as a

woman in a wheelchair pushed herself with one hand while viewing the garden.

"Everyone has a story of heroism, if given the chance to tell it. Don't you think, dear? For some, it's smelling roses, no matter what the challenge. For others, it's making a life without the ones we love."

She thought about Martine. Living apart from her son as she did must have been excruciating. A brave soul indeed.

"There's something that's been bothering me about my visit to Chugg Muehler's home. There were no pictures of Rigg. I guess maybe it's too painful for Martine."

She put her head on Leo's shoulder, listening to the hum of the air conditioner and allowed her eyes to close, just for a minute.

"Cheese and crackers!" She sat up and stared at her handsome husband. "Leo, there was something sitting on that mantle that shouldn't have been there!"

"How are you doing on this fine day, Mrs. Reed? It's good to see you out and about on your own."

She turned to see Trent, Leo's nurse, standing behind them. He was a tall man with broad shoulders and a broader smile. He was her favorite person, next to Leo, in the whole facility.

"It is, isn't it? This is my first time out alone. Not at my doctor's insistence, but my daughter's. You know what I'm talking about, right?"

Trent had his share of run-ins with Sophia. He was never doing anything right, as far as she was concerned.

"Oh, yes. It's good she's concerned about you, though. I doubt my folks would care if I fell off the face of the earth tomorrow."

She dropped her hands into her lap. In all of their months of friendship, she'd never asked about his family. "Oh, Trent. Tell me, why don't they value you for the shining example of a human that you are?"

He pulled up a chair and sat down beside them. "It's probably too long to tell you now. They thought I should do something more manly. *'Nurses are all women, son.'* Day after day. They didn't even come to my graduation. I haven't seen them since."

"My friend, Feather, has overcome similar circumstances. You have to make your own family. Once that circle is complete, you'll feel better than you did with those Negative Nellies."

Trent smiled and rubbed his dry hands together. "That's nice of you, Mrs. Reed. I do have a great group of friends and they act as family for me. It's good to see you here again. We were all worried about you after your fall."

"Thank you, dear." She patted his back. "Yes, we are lucky to surround ourselves with good people."

Gemini's eyes widened.

"Is there something wrong, Mrs. Reed?"

"Something just occurred to me. There's someone who isn't as lucky as us. She's got dangerous people around her and I need to help."

Trent dug into Gemini's usual container of

goodies and pulled out several bars. "Some for later," he explained sheepishly. "And some for my friends."

Chapter Twenty-Eight
FEATHER

"What brings you here today, Feather?" Jayden Ko leaned back in the leather chair, displaying her multi-colored brushstroke catsuit with pride.

"You're an empath, aren't you? Don't you know already?" she snapped. "Sorry, that was uncalled for. I haven't been sleeping much." Feather hadn't even bothered to style her hair before she left home. That's how little she cared about today.

"Yesterday, I told my staff I was selling the business. It was a hard day and I guess that affected my already-poor sleep.

No! You can't! We won't work for a stranger!

"Oh?" Jayden picked up a pen from the desk in front of her and twirled it in her fingers. "I'm sorry for your discomfort."

"Yes. I've come to a decision. More than one, actually." Feather cleared her throat and mustered all the strength she had. "I've got too much on my plate. I don't think I can work with Tag Junior anymore. To be honest, I think he's not gifted at all. He just wanted to make sure I wasn't dating his brother for his money. That's been proven to his satisfaction."

A hint of a smile crossed Jayden's face. "I see."

Feather felt the hairs on her arms rising.

She knows all.

"Jayden Ko, you've been playing me." The more she thought about it, the more sense it made. "You've been playing me," she said again, this time with a full understanding.

Feather stood and crossed her arms. "I'm done with your silly little tests. I don't need your group. You can find someone else to help you get your certification back. They can make friends with the ghost and make themselves the face of your organization. Whoever that person is, it won't be me. Tag probably wasn't going to give you money anyway. None of them can be trusted. None except Tug."

"Feather, please sit down. I'd like to explain."

"I'll give you five minutes. But then I'm out of here for good."

"I'll only need four." Jayden leaned forward. "Do you know why I took this position?"

Feather shrugged.

"Because I wanted to belong. There aren't many people in the world who wear catsuits and even fewer who are paranormal investigators. I'm an anomaly. I found this group and I knew I fit. My life is better because of these people."

"That's fine for you, but–"

Jayden held her hand up. "You need them too. Tag Junior came to us because he assumed you were a member. He coerced us into seeking you out. All of that is true. But don't you wonder where his paranormal ideas came from?"

Feather gulped. It was Rigg Muehler who had the gift, not his father. She didn't feel like sharing that piece of information though.

"You and I found our place. But whoever this person is, hasn't. They are still wandering alone with only Tag Junior to show them the way. Do we want to leave someone out there alone without the right support?"

The last thing Feather wanted was to inflict pain on Rigg, but he wasn't open to help. "I know who it is, and they aren't open to help, at least not from me. I think that brings my services to your organization to an end. I'm sorry about the donation from the Muehler family."

Feather rose to leave.

"You're a good person, Feather Jones. You're helping someone in need. And who knows, maybe Tag Junior is also in need of a listening ear."

Feather reached for the doorknob.

"Oh, and Feather? Have you figured out what Julianne wants you to know? I've not been able to make any sense of it. Of course, it was your message all along, not mine."

"You know who it is?" Feather sat back down. "What else aren't you telling me, Jayden?"

Jayden smiled politely and folded her hands across her middle. "I could be coy and ask what you mean, but I think we're beyond that. Julianne told me she would only speak to you. Kind of like Tag Junior. Doesn't that tell you something? These beings, one dead, one alive, are drawn to you for some purpose."

Feather's head was reeling. If Julianne was the spirit in her dreams, it was telling her to slow down. Jayden's message was the complete opposite.

"You don't need my gifts at all. You've got all of the tools to solve this yourself. I've been keeping this from Tug and it's tearing me up inside. I have way too much on my plate as it is, which you should also know, but here we are, having another conversation filled with puzzle pieces. I'm over it, Jayden."

She felt the hairs on her arms rise for the second time today. Instinctively, she glanced at Jayden to see if she felt anything different in the room.

"Yes, I know," Jayden said quietly. "Ask her what she wants."

The house of turns is a façade.

"Yes, we've established it's the laundromat. What is hiding underneath the laundromat?"

There was a sense of relief in knowing she could speak out loud to the spirit around Jayden without any judgment. "Tell me now, because I'm not coming back no matter how many of my dreams you haunt."

The house of turns is a façade.

The voice was louder, demanding and almost threatening.

Go away!

"I'm doing exactly as you instructed. If you have more to say to Feather, now is the time. What is this façade you're referring to?"

Feather was shocked to hear Jayden speaking to the spirit.

Jayden nodded. "She's been haunting my dreams too. You can't just walk out on us now. We need to figure out exactly what she's saying so we can both have peace!"

"What is it, Julianne? I found your note. Someone was blackmailing you before your death. Do you want me to find them?"

The tension in the air eased and the spirit was gone.

"I promise you, Feather, if you find one answer, you'll find them all. Don't give up on us yet. Please?"

There was a knock at the door and a woman entered tenuously. "Ms. Ko? Your ten o-clock will be delayed. Traffic."

Chapter Twenty-Nine

GEMINI

Martine Muehler stood under five feet. This in and of itself wasn't unusual, but amongst the tall, broad shouldered Muehler family, with the exception of Mitzi, she seemed out of place.

Her delicate presentation made it hard to imagine her standing up to a powerful woman like Mitzi Muehler.

"Thank you for meeting me today, Mrs. Muehler."

Martine blinked her dark eyes several times and gazed around the room. "There's no one else with you?" Her voice was tiny and delicate, just like her body. She could blow over if the right customer came barreling through the door.

Gemini cut her marionberry pie into tiny pieces. She wanted to make this conversation last as long as she could. Martine nibbled on her salad, but pushed the plate away after a few bites.

Gemini glanced around Four Cups, finding the

usual afternoon crowd—the two men playing cards, a woman who read books on her phone, and the couple who met for late lunch on Thursdays.

"The coast is clear. If you'll tell me who you want to avoid, I can make sure to watch for them."

Martine, as if snapped out of a trance, eyed Gemini with suspicion. "Who says I'm trying to avoid someone? Did they send you?"

"No one sent me, dear. This family has really got you twisted, hasn't it? They have no right!"

Gemini's heart ached. This poor, lost soul put her trust in the wrong family.

"I'm a bit of an amateur detective and I'm trying to help your son out of a pickle." She wasn't sure if she should mention any more than that. Chugg may have kept the details from her to avoid a breakdown.

"You're helping my Rigg?" Her bright eyes brimmed with tears. "How is he?"

"He's struggling. He doesn't fit in at the fancy boarding school he attends. Just like all teenagers, he has to find his own way."

"I forget he's that old. The last time I saw him, he was in diapers." She picked a piece of lettuce off her plate and ate a tiny bite, chewing quickly, like a rabbit.

"Yes, I know about that situation. It's terrible. That family should not have cut you out. It's not right for a mother to lose her son like that."

This was the point at which she hoped Martine would jump in with her side of the story. They ate in silence for a few minutes, Gemini waiting patiently for information that wasn't coming.

"Say, I have an idea. I'd decided to see Rigg before. I can contact him again and the two of you can chat in the park. None of the Muehlers would have to know."

Martine's chewing came to an abrupt halt. "Oh, they'd know. You underestimate the Meuhler dynasty's ability to sniff out deceit. It must be genetic; they all have it. Thank you for your offer, but for now, things need to remain as they are."

It struck Gemini as peculiar that she was so quick to turn her down. A chance to see Rigg after all these years had to be an exciting prospect. Just a few minutes earlier she'd been in tears at the mention of his name.

"All right. You can always change your mind. Now, to the matter at hand." She took another bite of pie, savoring the not-too-sweet flavor and opened her purse.

"During the course of my investigation, I found this photo. That's your cousin, Diego Betz?"

She slid a copy of the wedding photo from Tag Junior's mantle across the table.

Martine studied the picture. "That was my wedding day. At the time, I thought it was the best day of my life. My first warning should have been when Tag's grandmother greeted me moments before I walked down the aisle. She said, *'Martine, we know you trapped Tag Junior with your pregnancy and then the prenup. But I'll be watching you. When you least expect it, I'm going to make sure you pay for what you've done to our family.'* The more I thought about it, the more I realized, this family is a business. They aren't interested in connections at all. Everyone, that is, except for Chugg."

She stared at Gemini as if trying to bore a hole through her chest. Gemini adjusted her striped, powder blue shirt uncomfortably.

"Sorry, you were asking about my cousin. Yes, that's Diego. We were always close. He warned me not to get involved with this family. He was always looking out for me." She pushed the picture away and picked a cherry tomato from her salad.

Gemini watched in fascination as she opened her tiny mouth far enough to engulf the plump tomato.

"Do you know that he was murdered? It happened in the same school where your son, Rigg, was attending. Rigg was the last person to see him alive."

Gemini braced for whatever reaction Martine might have. The way Chugg talked, she was on the edge of a complete mental breakdown.

Instead, she took a tiny piece of cheese from the top of the salad and popped it in her mouth. She licked one finger, and then the next. "This place is wonderful! I'll have to tell Chugg about it!"

"Martine, did you hear what I said? Your son witnessed a murder."

As she'd learned with Leo's care, there was a fine line between making your point and causing distress. Maybe she'd reached that with Martine.

She nodded and smiled. "Of course. He's a

Muehler and they don't let anyone with that name go to prison. He'll be fine."

Gemini's eyes widened. "And what about your cousin Diego? Did you know he was in contact with your mother-in-law, Mitzi?"

She sighed, delicately. "He was a sweet man. I'm sure Mitzi enjoyed his company."

"Do you think Chugg knew they were in contact? Would that have upset him?"

Abruptly, Martine leaned forward and grabbed Gemini's hand so hard she pinched the skin.

"Ouch!" Gemini yanked hard until she was free from Martine's grip. "I'm sorry for your pain, Martine, but I'm not the cause of it."

Howard promised to return in twenty minutes, after he'd been to the hardware store for more patio screws. It had been at least thirty.

"She's here," Martine whispered in a low, menacing voice. "If she finds out I've left my room, she'll be furious. I'm going to the bathroom. Tell her I left."

Martine jumped up, on a dead run for the door marked, "She" at the back of the restaurant.

Stunned, Gemini brought her phone out and texted Howard. "911. Not kidding." That ought to bring him.

She heard clacking heels, feet that meant business coming up behind her. It wasn't Patsy. She had a slow, steady gait. She remembered when Tug was selling self-defense tools, he gave her a whistle that was as loud as a train. Fishing around in her purse, she grabbed it with two fingers and prepared to turn around and blow it in the face of this unwanted stranger.

She felt the person's warm breath on her neck and her fingers curled around the whistle.

"You're looking for Martine, but she's gone. She didn't want to deal with you today. I had to deliver some distressing news and she'd like her privacy. If you don't leave now, I'm prepared to make a scene."

Gemini sat erect, not daring to turn her head.

"I gave her strict instructions not to leave the premises after she took her meds. It's a real bug-a-boo to me when patients disobey instructions."

Gemini gasped and pushed herself out of the booth, turning to see a familiar face.

"Cheese and biscuits! Skye? What on earth are you doing here?"

Her former nurse raised one eyebrow. "I could ask the same of you. When I was dismissed, I gave you strict instructions to rest every day at this time."

"I don't need to rest. I'm not an infant nor an invalid. People need me."

Realizing she no longer had a hold over Gemini, Skye attempted to move beyond her, toward the bathroom.

Gemini stepped in front of her. "No. I'll not allow it. This poor woman needs some breathing room. Her goon of a boyfriend hired you, no doubt, as a bodyguard as well as a medicinal dispensary. Well, you can go home and report you observed Martine having lunch with a friend and she was relaxed and happy."

Skye huffed and stomped her foot. "Gemini Reed, you were the most disagreeable patient I've ever dealt with. Don't think I didn't know about the times you were in my care and snuck out. This isn't over. Once I tell Chugg about this, he'll find more people to watch her. This family has endless resources."

At an impasse, Skye tried one more time to cross her, but Gemini stood firm.

"He may very well send his goons next time. But that's not today. There's only you and a little old lady. Oh, and the security cameras," Gemini pointed above her head, to a black square in the corner. "I suggested they install these after a robbery. I'd hate it if they were used to prove you assaulted me."

This time, Skye was truly out of options. She stormed out of the café, slamming the door in her dramatic exit.

Gemini knocked on the bathroom door. "Martine? The coast is clear. Skye is gone."

Slowly, the door opened, and Martine appeared, her makeup smeared from crying.

"Oh, thank you, Gemini. I feel like I'm being smothered. Ever since my cousin died, they've kept me locked up in my room. When they hired this militant nurse, she started monitoring everything, and I do mean–"

"Bowel movements. Yes, I know. She was my nurse for two excruciating weeks." Gemini rolled her eyes. "Now, we need to talk about how we're going to get you out of this prison. I believe Chugg killed your cousin and now may be trying to control you to keep your money."

Martine's face displayed a look of amusement. "You think Chugg might hurt me? He's not the type."

"You're being medicated, Martine. It's how they control smart women like us. Leave it to me and Tug. We'll save you."

Chapter Thirty

FEATHER

Tug took one of Gemini's famous peanut butter brownies from the plastic tub and put it on a plate, one of ten mismatched plates Feather found at an auction. Feather shook her head. "You're going to eat that entire thing before it hits the table again. Why are you bothering with the plate?"

"If one of your clients comes in, I want to make sure I don't embarrass you." He opened his mouth wide and placed the brownie, whole, in his mouth, wiping the crumbs from his hands. "Are you going to take me up on my offer?"

"To investigate Jayden? I'm not sure that's going to help us."

"Feath, she's not being honest with you. She says she knows everything there is to know, and yet she still can't figure out what this spirit wants. And besides that," he shoved another entire brownie into his mouth as he spoke. "You discovered her last name is Ko. That family—"

"Someone with that name runs Ko Industries, the largest supplier of natural foods on the west coast, I know." Feather studied his face, always happy to see his devotion to her displayed with ease. "It doesn't mean she's related to them."

Tug chased his brownies with a glass of cashew milk, which he downed in one long gulp.

"If you and Gemini have that kind of time, go ahead and check her out. But don't let anyone catch you, and if you do, please, please, don't mention my name!"

"Agreed." Tug took a third brownie and devoured it in the same manner as the last two. "What else can I do to lighten your load? After all of this is over, you need to let go of something else, Feath."

"I went to the bank yesterday," Stevie-the-new-girl announced as she walked in carrying a bowl of purple-hued highlight solution.

"Oh? Are you having financial difficulties, Stevie-the-new-girl? I could help..." Feather offered. She'd made loans to employees before. They were always grateful and repaid them as quickly as possible.

Stevie-the-new-girl shook her head as she rinsed the bowl. "No, thanks. I was looking into a loan to buy this place." She removed her gloves and wiped her hands.

Feather and Tug exchanged a look of surprise.

"I didn't know you were interested. It's a big responsibility!"

"I have a business degree, and I went to a conflict resolution training seminar. Everything else will come with time."

"I hadn't thought of that," Feather said uncomfortably. As much as she liked Stevie-the-new-girl, she was so new to the world of styling she might not be able to handle all of it.

"Anyway, it was a nice dream, but the bank wouldn't lend me any money. I still have a car loan, and they think I'm too young."

Feather let out a sigh of relief. "Some time in the future, Stevie-the-new-girl. Don't give up."

When Stevie-the-new-girl remained planted in place, Feather asked, "Did you need something else?"

"One of your clients is here. He says you told him he could come any time."

Feather frowned. "I don't think I've said that to anyone. I'm booked solid for the next month."

"He said you'd say that too. And he wants me to remind you that he's paying handsomely for your time."

Her face felt hot and she was afraid to stand without falling over.

"I know who it is. Tell him I'll be out in a minute."

She watched Stevie-the-new-girl leave then looked at Tug with fear in her eyes. "You won't be happy."

"You're right, I'm not. Who thinks they can waltz

in whenever they want? Stay here, Feath. I'll take care of this jerk."

"No, Tug! Wait!" she called in vain as Tug stormed out the door of the Friendship Room.

She wasn't entirely sure she wanted to stop him. The burden of keeping secrets from him had been too great. He deserved to know the truth.

Just sitting there, she could feel palpitations in her chest again and her mind was spinning. Her whole body was shaking so badly her teeth rattled in her head.

The hairs on her arms rose.

Turmoil threatens to explode the portal.

There was a scream, and someone yelled for Feather.

"Tug! No!"

In the front of the salon, Tug was on the floor with his hands around his brother's throat. Several women in black salon capes were standing around them yelling at them to stop. Stevie-the-new-girl was attempting to separate them.

Feather leaned down and whispered in Tug's ear.

"He's not worth it. Let him go and look at a person who really loves you."

He looked up at her, suddenly broken from a trance-like state. "Feath?"

With Tug's grip loosened, Tag Junior pushed himself up and shoved his brother away. Both men had bloodied their noses and welts appeared in various places on their bodies.

One of the caped women with rows of small, pink

curlers in her head handed Tag Junior a cup of water and the towel from around her neck.

After drinking the entire cup and shoving it back in the woman's hand, Tag Junior straightened his expensive shirt collar, unaware that it was covered in his brother's blood. "You're going to hear from my lawyer. Nothing has changed about you. But I shouldn't be surprised. You always thought with your fists instead of your brain."

Feather put her hand on Tug's chest, willing him to be still. "What are you doing here, Tag? We didn't have a meeting scheduled for today."

Tug looked at them both with hurt in his eyes. "You've been seeing my brother and you didn't tell me?"

"You know how to pick 'em, eh, brother?" Tag Junior smirked. "Feather and I have had several meetings. We even sat in an empty theatre together. She never once mentioned you."

Tug lurched at him again. This time, Feather moved in between them. "You know that's not true, Tag."

She shoved Tug gently to create space between the warring brothers.

"He's making this into something it's not, Tug. I've been helping him with his abilities, though we both know that was a ruse to get to me."

"I don't understand. Why would you keep this from me? We don't have secrets."

"He blackmailed the P.I.N.K. organization into

finding me. He said he'd give them a large check if I worked in secret with him. I figured out pretty early on that he was scamming me."

Tug rubbed his neck and glared at his brother. "Not surprised. He's never had a truthful bone in his body."

"I thought I would invite you both for dinner, since I have plenty of income from my position in Muehler Industries. Now I can see it was a stupid idea. This Neanderthal shouldn't be in public. At least not when he's not in a zoo exhibit," Tag Junior snarled.

Feather held tightly to Tug's waist, hoping he wouldn't have another urge to hit his brother. She wasn't strong enough to stop him. Another customer handed her a towel, and she reached up and blotted his nose.

"I highly doubt that's the reason you're here, brother. Tell me what's going on and why you're standing in a beauty shop that's far below your standards."

"I had another vision."

Feather turned abruptly toward Tug. "Can you wait for me in the back?"

"I'm not leaving you alone with him," Tug whispered. "You already said he was making this up."

"Give me five minutes. I've got the Permanent Gang out here watching. They won't let anything happen to me."

Reluctantly, he walked back to the room and Feather returned to Tag Junior.

"Your son can come talk to me about his visions any time he wants. I guess it's a good thing that you care enough about him to find out about his gift."

Tag Junior's puffy eyes made him appear more intimidating as he placed his hands on his hips.

There was a heaviness in the air, and no one moved, as if trapped by the weight of it.

The fear she'd felt when they first met was gone. Tug knew all about their weird relationship and she'd outed Tag Junior as a fraud. He was a small, bitter man.

It took a moment to reach the surface, but a giggle erupted. She couldn't stop it. The thought of Tag Junior standing there, swollen, bloody and rumpled, surrounded by ladies in curlers was too much.

"What are you laughing at?" There was hurt in his voice. "I don't find any of this funny."

Feather wiped her eyes on her shirt, by now a solid stream of liquid laughter erupting from them. "I'm sorry. You've been playing such a silly game of pretend. You didn't fool me, and your brother thinks even less of you now than he ever did, if that's possible. What did this get you?"

The other women snickered, and the mood of the room lightened considerably.

"You don't know what you're talking about." Tag Junior brushed his shirt, removing nonexistent debris. "I'd like to speak with you in private, Miss Jones. It's important."

"No, I don't think so. Our relationship is officially over."

Feather pivoted to walk away, and he caught her arm. She shook him loose, feeling angry enough to take him down herself. "You can find the door. If not, I'll be forced to call your brother out here. He won't escort you out in a civilized manner."

"Rigg told me all about your meeting. We don't keep secrets. Tug was there too."

She turned around, caught completely off guard. "Why would you drag him into this? That's a horrible thing to do to a child. Your problems with Tug have nothing to do with–"

"Everything in my life is done for his benefit." His eyes jumped from one client to the next. "I'd really like to discuss this in private."

"If it will remove you from my life permanently, all right." Feather turned and gestured to the closest employee. "Stevie-the-new-girl, will you make sure everyone is taken care of? Bring everyone a refreshment from the Friendship Room, if they want. I'm going to step out in front with Mr. Muehler for EXACTLY five minutes."

She hoped Stevie-the-new-girl would understand her emphasis as a message to notify Tug if she was gone any longer.

"Yes, you bet, Feather. Five minutes. C'mon, ladies, let's get you settled."

Feather followed Tag Junior outside. She felt

comfort in knowing it was broad daylight and there were many people passing them on the sidewalk.

"Okay, spill it. The clock is ticking." She folded her arms across her chest and leaned against the brick building.

"I wish we could go somewhere more private."

"This is all you get. I'm going to Jayden as soon as we're done and telling her everything. Your money, I'm sure, will still be welcome, but your name will not."

"I...this...it's very hard to tell you this." He ran his hands through his thick hair just as Tug did when he was nervous.

"I can see that," Feather replied, surprised that she actually could see his discomfort. He did actually possess regular human emotions.

"I came to this group for two reasons. Yes, I did want to check you out. Tug has been making motions to rejoin the family and we always check out prospective interlopers." He sighed so loud the couple walking by carrying their infant turned and stared at him for a moment before continuing on.

"My son, Rigg, has always been different. I've known that since he was five. I sent him to art class and he came home with a painting of my grandfather from nineteen forty-six. The other kids made flowers and trees."

Feather felt the hairs on her arms rising. "Go on."

"He's such a good kid. I always encouraged him, no matter what the teachers said. That's why I sent him to the Smiley Academy. I wanted him to have a fresh start, to feel like he fit somewhere. When that didn't happen, I was beside myself with worry."

She remembered the conversation Howard and Gemini had with Rigg. They mentioned he was uncomfortable returning to his school.

"Rigg, my son, has a..."

"A gift. He hears the dearly departed." Feather looked at him with satisfaction. "You've got to stop making him feel like it's a disease. He's really fortunate."

He knows more. Ask him.

Tag cocked his head to the side and squinted. "I'm still not sure this is real. I took him to a therapist who said he was making up people to get attention."

"Is that what you think I do? Because, believe me, I get plenty of attention without making up stories." Feather tapped the side of her head. "They talk to me."

"Oh. Right." He didn't seem convinced, but continued on. "He waited outside the door of the teacher's lounge. I'm not talking about the day of the murder. The week before, he was trying to find a quiet place to...talk to spirits. He was sitting there when he heard his name come up. He peaked through the door and saw Diego Betz talking to another man. I grilled him until he admitted he heard that man's name. It was my Uncle Chugg."

"Really?" Feather replied noncommittally. "I wonder why he would be there?"

"He killed Diego Betz. I'm sure of it. Martine's last

payout from her prenup comes this month. Diego must've asked Martine for money."

"Why are you telling me this now?"

"I'd like you to work with my son. He may be able to help us solve the murder."

Chapter Thirty-One

GEMINI

"I just can't get over it. That woman turns up everywhere. It's true what they say—once you've allowed an evil force into your life, it follows you forever." Gemini moved the cooled batch of Tug Bars to her kitchen table. She was more than happy to give Tug and Olive that space to work in, and pleased they asked her to help.

"It is a little weird, your nurse right there in the restaurant. Some kind of conspiracy, you think? There's no such thing as a coincidence. Someone is after you. Makes you wonder what kind of evil lurks below the surface of our sweet little town, doesn't it?" Olive replied, slurping her chocolate shake.

"It's not that bad, Olive. But I do need to figure out how to get Martine away from Chugg. He's drugging her and once she gets her final settlement from Tag Junior, I'm afraid she'll have outlived her usefulness to him, and maybe to the rest of the family as well."

"Did I ever tell you about my family? Most of us have got a hook at the end of our noses." Olive curled her pointer finger and placed it at the end of her nose for example.

"Oh?" Gemini was only half-listening as she drizzled a cream cheese icing over the bars. "Your husband's side was a little homely?"

"Oh, my family, not the Thomas family of my late husband, rest his soul, but the Ogalbindersmidt clan. Every single one of us has a birthmark right here." Olive pointed her spatula at her forehead, tapping dead center.

Gemini leaned forward, as far as she could with the counter in the way. "Oh, my. Would you look at that? Right in the middle of your forehead. Olive, I never noticed before!"

Heart-shaped, it was a discreet light brown spot in between her eyebrows, hidden amongst several age spots.

"The bigger question is your maiden name. That's quite the moniker!"

"My father hated it. He encouraged all of us girls to get married lickety-split so we wouldn't be saddled with that for the rest of our lives. He was old-fashioned —he went through the phonebook and found eligible men with surnames under eight letters."

"Your father was no-nonsense. Were you given the

opportunity to choose from short-named bachelors at least?"

Olive nodded vigorously. "We all were. My older sister, Oraline, really liked Spunk Trot, but he had an overbearing mother. She moved right on past him to Phil Shan. Daddy wanted the best for us. He would have cut off his right arm if we needed it."

"You've got me thinking, Olive. The thing that concerns me most is Martine's reaction to Rigg's situation. She wasn't the least bit concerned about her son. Maybe you get that way after such a lengthy separation. Could be the way she copes."

Gemini took a long drink of her ice water and set it on her coffee table, the only space still available.

"Could be the fact that Chugg has kept her isolated for so long she's completely lost touch with the real world. But it's worrisome. She showed more reaction to Skye's arrival than the news that her son was the prime suspect in a murder."

"What did she say, exactly, when Skye showed up?" Olive slurped the last of her chocolate shake and held the glass up to her face, allowing enough time for the last bit of chocolate and whipped cream to slide down the middle.

As Olive turned to put her glass down, she knocked a cookie sheet filled with uncooked bars to the floor. Gemini reacted as quickly as possible, but she missed.

"You two need a larger space to work," she

muttered as she picked up the dough. "This is getting ridiculous."

Olive scooped everything in the trash and turned to Gemini, hands on hips. "You're not wrong about that. You were about to tell me what Martine said when Skye walked in?"

"Just that she needed to leave." Gemini concentrated on her broom, sweeping all the brown crumbs off her linoleum. She was feeling much better, but it was still going to hurt to get on her hands and knees and wash the floor. Something she would never admit to Olive.

"If it were up to me, I'd buy these kids a mansion. I've offered. But you know those two, they think they have to earn their own way."

Olive shook her head and broke one bar into two pieces, setting one precariously close to the edge of the sink for Gemini. She popped the other in her mouth.

"Not quite sweet enough." She wrote the comment down on the recipe, along with the words, "add more dates."

"Olive, I've decided that we need to rescue Martine from the compound where she's being held. The poor dear, she's overmedicated and confused. And they've got Nurse Nightmare caring for her. It's intolerable and I want her out before the money hits her account."

"I'm in, Gemini! Just have Tug pick me up before seven. That's when they turn all the lights out and I won't be able to see my way out the front door."

"I haven't even told you yet what we're doing!"

"Doesn't matter. I look forward to our time together. I'll dress up or pretend to be a goat if that's what you want."

Gemini giggled. "You're a treasure, Olive. I'll let you know. Tug and I have another project to complete first."

"I just had a thought." Olive banged her spatula against her opposite hand, spraying crumbs all over Gemini's freshly swept floor.

"We could rescue Martine and tie up that nurse. You could tell her everything you wanted to say when she was here."

"I just remembered something, Olive. You asked what Martine said when she saw Skye. She said, 'She can't see me here with you.' How did she know Skye was my acquaintance?"

Chapter Thirty-Two

GEMINI

"That's an impressive shiner. I'll refrain from asking what happened, though you know Feather will tell me anyway." Gemini tried not to stare, but the discolored surface of Tug's normally model-perfect face disturbed her.

"I'll tell you, I promise. Just not now, when our focus is on Jayden's secret life." Tug adjusted the security badge around his neck, the one Howard requested from his top-secret IT person.

"Just promise me that you'll get it checked out."

"Feather made an appointment for me. Next Tuesday."

The two of them held hands as they approached the tall marble desk.

"May I help you?"

"Grant Muehler. I'm one of those lucky guys who normally works from home. My grandma is visiting from Texas and wanted to see where I work. I told her I'd love to show her around."

Gemini winked. "Got in yesterday for a short visit. I'm so gosh-darned proud of my Grant. First thing I says to my boy, ya'll gonna show me your building? And like the good grandson he is, he said, 'Course I am, Grannie'!"

A tall thin man on the other side of the reception desk stared at Tug. "Goodness, what happened to your eye? Working from home must be treacherous."

Tug smiled and winced when the crinkling of his cheek caused pain. "Had to let my dog out last night and I tripped over the end table."

The man held out his hand expectantly and Tug removed the badge from around his neck and handed it to him.

It beeped when it was scanned, working as smoothly as all of Howard's badges did.

He handed the badge back, along with one that read, 'Visitor,' for Gemini.

"I hope you'll get that checked out. You never know when something is broken."

"Next Tuesday."

They headed for the elevator, still hand in hand. Once they were inside, they dropped hands, and both breathed a sigh of relief.

"That went much easier than I thought it would!" Gemini exclaimed.

"Please thank Howard for the rush order. I took the liberty of hacking their system to find Jayden's office. It's on the top floor. That part was pretty easy, but getting in to see her might take more finesse."

"Don't worry, Tug. I'm prepared."

As the elevator doors opened, Gemini marveled at the floor-to-ceiling glass. Every step she took turned the floor a different color, making the fact that she was walking across the heads of people on floor number ten less weird.

People buzzed by them as they walked.

"Jayden Ko, CEO. This is it, Tug," Gemini whispered, motioning to the only completely solid wood door in view. "You might have mentioned the fact that she is the boss. Just a small detail."

As Tug raised his hand to knock on the door, they both heard someone clearing their throat and turned to see a stern-faced suit wearing a SECURITY badge standing behind them.

"This area is restricted. Your badge gives you clearance for floors two through eight. I'm going to have to ask you to leave."

Gemini smiled, winking at the security guard. It worked once before.

"My grandson had some important documents to deliver to Ms. Ko."

The security guard held out his hand.

"Oh, no. They must be hand-delivered," Gemini insisted.

The guard, unwavering in his stance, pointed toward the elevators.

"Come on, Grandma. We'll have to see her later,"

Tug said, taking Gemini's arm. As they turned to walk back to the elevator, they heard a voice from behind the door.

"Homer, I've been expecting them. Please let them in."

"I...um," Tug stuttered.

"You see? She's been expecting us," Gemini said with a hint of pride.

"Ms. Ko, I'm not so sure..." Homer viewed the man with the shiner and his grandmother skeptically.

"Escort them in, Homer," the voice reiterated. "They are my guests."

"Okay, boss lady." Homer used his badge to unlock the door and ushered them inside.

A woman wearing a shiny, black and orange catsuit, a black wig and cat-eye glasses stood to greet them.

"Tug and Gemini! Right on schedule!" She motioned for them to sit in clear plastic chairs with lavender cushions.

Gemini eased herself into the chair, expecting pain from the odd angle and unforgiving surface. Instead, she found it surprisingly comfortable. "Oh, this is delightful!"

"Isn't it? A friend in New York made them for me. We went to college together and he's now one of the premiere furniture designers in the world."

"How did you know we were coming?" Tug asked suspiciously. "And how did you know our names?"

Jayden sat down at the desk and clasped her hands in front of her. "I could say that I keep track of all the new recruits and who they consort with. I could also say that Feather has been forthcoming about her relationships and who means what to her. I could say those things, but they would be lies."

Tug shook his head. "Games. Feather warned me you spoke in riddles."

"I have a knack for knowing things," Jayden replied matter-of-factly.

Gemini eased back into the chair, leaning her head against the headrest, still marveling at the technology. "Miss Ko, is there something sinister happening here? Is that why you never told Feather about your position?"

Jayden laughed heartily. "I forgot, you're an amateur detective. You're always on the lookout for people doing spy things. I love your energy, Gemini!"

Tug growled. "We're not interested in playing, Jayden. What do you know and why do you want us here?"

"I knew you were on your way here, after figuring out that I was hiding something from Feather. Lots of somethings."

Gemini's eyes narrowed, even though her body was still in a reclined position, staring at the ceiling. "Why are you putting Feather through all of this for Tag Junior's money, when you have plenty of your own to fund your organization?"

"She has to make this journey. My money would only hinder her."

"Good grief." Tug looked up at the clear ceiling, where pigeons fought over a piece of bread. "I think you're a fraud. You talk in circles until people eventually figure things out on their own. Did I get that right, Jayden?"

Jayden smiled, unaffected by his harsh words. "It would make it much easier to understand me if that were true. You've got a journey of your own to make, Tug Meuhler. You need to come to terms with your family, or there will be more black eyes in your future."Tug grasped the arm rests and attempted to lurch at Jayden, but Gemini put her hand on his chest, stopping him.

"I'm a rather simple woman, Miss Ko. I'd like to ask you some simple questions and receive straightforward answers."

"Mrs. Reed, you're anything but simple. You're conflicted about your feelings for your next door neighbor, and—"

Gemini's face turned crimson. "Let's just get to it. First question, why are you working with Tag Junior? How does that benefit Feather?"

Jayden leaned forward and clasped her hands in front of her, her expertly manicured red-and-white nails sparkling. "That's actually two questions. I'm working with Tag Junior so that Feather can facilitate a reunion between him and his brother."

Tug shook his head vigorously. "Not a chance.

This shiner," he pointed to his face, "is from our first meeting. The next time, he won't be so lucky."

"Now you understand my use of riddles. It avoids this kind of response."

"Next question," Gemini continued. "What about this spirit in the laundromat? I don't believe for a minute that Feather is the only person who can communicate with it. What's the story?"

Jayden smiled. "You're very perceptive. I'm afraid I'll have to defer to Feather on this one. She'll realize very soon and you both will be the first to learn of her discovery."

Tug stood and held his hand out for Gemini. "We need to leave. This woman is making me mad, and I don't want to say something that will upset Feather."

"You have more questions though," Jayden said, almost pleadingly. "I'd like to answer as many as I can."

Tug made no effort to sit, but nodded. "Let's get on with it. Instead of us wasting time asking, why don't you just tell us."

"Okay, let's see." She stroked her chin with one long finger. "Gemini, you'll find a neighbor in distress soon, and–"

Tug leaned over her desk and pounded it with his fists. "No more riddles!"

Jayden jumped, unsettled by the sound.

"What, you didn't know I was going to do that?" Tug asked, amused. "There are still a few surprises in the world."

Jayden's eyes narrowed. "There are, Tug Muehler.

Including your connection to Gemini's troublesome nurse."

Gemini and Tug stared at each other in disbelief.

"I don't know what you're talking about," Tug replied dismissively.

"Did you know that Skye Baker came to our city at my behest? She spent months working in our labs. I brought her here from the east coast to help us in our development of edible plastics. It's going to help the environment when people can eat their sandwich wrappers, don't you think?"

"What does that have to do with nursing? It's an odd career move for a medical professional," Gemini remarked.

Jayden nodded. "I can understand why you'd think that. But she monitored our control group. She took their blood after they ate the wrappers and made sure no one would come to physical harm. For that, she was paid three times her nursing salary."

"Why did she leave?" Tug asked. "That sounds like a job with a lot of perks."

"You might say she did it under duress. We'd recently discovered she was selling our formulas to the Muehler Company."

"My family doesn't make edible plastics," Tug scorned. "You'll have to come up with something better than that."

"I'm sorry you aren't in contact with your family. They could verify everything I've said. We let her go.

Well, that's not quite correct. Can I let you two in on a little secret?"

Gemini wasn't sure this person was trustworthy. So far, she hadn't brought harm to Feather, but she was too smooth, too polished. She nodded reluctantly.

"Skye got herself into a sticky situation when I discovered her deceit. I spent ten years in the FBI, so she was no match for my skills." Jayden sighed, the first actual emotion she'd shown since they entered her office. "She begged not to be fired, so I made her a deal."

Tug's hand bounced on his leg like he was listening to his own private drum solo. "You told her to go and work for my family, sharing what you wanted her to share and in exchange, you wouldn't sue her for breach of contract."

"Yes, that's exactly what happened. But I'm surprised Tug hasn't come up with the rest of the story."

Tug, who was standing at the tall bank of windows overlooking the ocean, turned around. "What?"

"Skye's connection to the Muehlers. Why would she risk everything for that family? Come on, Tug. Think."

Anger welled up inside Gemini. It was one thing to play with the facts, but quite another to try and manipulate Tug. "She's toying with us, Tug. Let's go. We can find Skye's secrets on our own."

Jayden leaped up from her desk, exhibiting the catlike reflexes expected from someone wearing a tiger striped cat suit. "Don't go! I haven't told you the best part. You have to find Bryanna Potter for your next clue. Don't forget! Bryanna Potter."

Gemini paused, but Tug pulled on her elbow. "Come on, Gem. I don't want someone else to end up with a black eye."

Chapter Thirty-Three

FEATHER

"I'm glad your dad gave us this time together today." Feather smiled uncomfortably. She'd offered to meet with Rigg without having a plan of action.

"Yeah, I guess." He folded his arms across his chest, much more shut down than he was that day in the park.

"You've been given a gift. I know it doesn't seem that way now, but the voices you hear are sometimes there to protect you."

"Right," he scoffed. "They were right there when my hands were duct taped together and I was thrown in the garbage. Really helpful."

"They warned you, but because you push them away, you thought it was just paranoia and you didn't listen."

Rigg sat up straight. "What did they say?"

"That's something you'll have to tell me."

Rigg closed his eyes and leaned his head back.

Feather took this opportunity to study his face. Same long eyelashes and strong jaw. He was every bit Tug's nephew.

He opened his eyes abruptly and looked at Feather. "They did tell me! Don't go to the Rec Center. I remember now!"

She wasn't positive that he was being honest, that maybe he was just trying to get this over with as soon as possible, but either way, he was acknowledging an important part of himself.

"Okay, good. Let's think of another time."

Rigg closed his eyes again.

"How about the day of the murder? What did you hear that day?"

His eyes moved rapidly from underneath those long lashes.

"Rigg? What are you thinking about?"

The hairs on Feather's arms stood.

He knows.

"What did you hear that day?" she repeated.

Rigg opened his eyes and grabbed his chair with both arms. "Nothing."

"It must be painful to relive–"

"I'm done for today. Tell my dad to pay you for whatever. I'm going to play video games."

He got up and left without so much as a goodbye, this boy she'd admired for his earnestness and sweet nature.

She was stunned by this unexpected turn of events.

He knows.

"I'm not dense," Feather snapped. "I've got to figure out another way into his mind."

* * *

"Tug, tell me about the day we met." Feather broke a biscotti into two pieces and placed one on his plate.

"What? You were there, Feath. I can't believe you don't remember," he replied mockingly. "Now I'm really hurt."

"Not after we met, but before. Tell me what led to our first meeting."

After her non-productive meeting with Rigg, it was time to switch gears and try to solve the other mystery, why there was a note left in the mirror at the *Fold 'Em and Go* for Tug.

"Oh, let's see. I got up and ate a big bowl of something sugary. Glad those days are done. I had a whole day planned of activities, but when I went to the dryer to get my workout clothes, everything was sopping wet."

"So what did you do next?"

"I took them to the laundromat and dried them."

"Umhm." Feather tried to keep her voice even. "You were drying your clothes in the laundromat. Did anything happen there?"

"This was a long time ago, Feath. I've got my business, and your business, and my brain is... oh, that's nice."

She stood and placed her fingers on either side of

his temples, rubbing gently. "Just close your eyes and think about it."

"Well, my mind is going places besides the laundromat," he joked.

She bent over his face and kissed him on the lips. "No, silly. Just concentrate on this for a minute. You're in the laundromat..."

"I'm in the laundromat, reading a magazine from the year 2000. Before we continue this, I think I should tell you something."

He sat upright and pulled her around his chair gently, until she was sitting on his lap.

"All of this talk about Julianne has me thinking. She and I used to ride our bikes to the gas station next door to the laundromat. We'd get candy and drinks. Small town activities, eh?" he chuckled.

"I knew she was hiding something from me, something big. One day, I said we should leave love notes for each other somewhere public, but somewhere no one else can see. I thought I was Mr. Romance. We did it a couple of times, but then we started drifting apart. I left notes for her at Jill's Pizza Pontoon behind the picture of the boat captain who died here. And she–"

"Left them in the mirror at the *Fold 'Em and Go*," Feather replied.

"How did you know that?"

"I have lots of sources, remember?" She tapped her head.

Julianne's note to Tug must've been left long before her death. To show him now, when she had no idea who the blackmailer was, would only serve to hurt him more. It also didn't explain why she was haunting that particular location.

"I'd like to find out exactly where Julianne died. I hope that won't upset you, babe."

"Not at all. But you asked me about the day we met, and the story is coming together. Would you like to hear it?"

Feather nodded.

"I stuck all of my clothes in the dryer and sat down. I think I'd been out late the night before and I was ready to zone out. But there was this older guy who kind of appeared out of nowhere. He started telling me about his illnesses. He asked if I worked out and I said yes. Then he asked if I was doing it that day. I said no, that I had too many errands to run and now my clothes had to dry..."

"That's good, babe," Feather encouraged. "Keep going."

"He said, 'The time is now, young man. Don't waste another minute. Dry your clothing and get to the gym for me. I'd give anything to have that body again.' I agreed with him, and it struck me that you never know what time you'll have, and that I should put my mind and body first."

It was just as she thought. There was a spirit who brought them together for the first time, maybe Julianne manifesting in human form as someone else. Tug was encouraged to be at the gym. Theirs wasn't a chance meeting.

Chapter Thirty-Four

GEMINI

"Fellows Art Gallery on Whipperwill Street. You can't miss it. It's got a bright green awning." Gemini pointed to the unimpressive building on the corner.

"Are you sure this is what you want to do? That woman may have been pulling your leg."

Howard parked the car and turned to her. "We don't know what we're getting ourselves into."

"After Jayden Ko told us she was our next clue, I went home and looked her up. Bryanna Potter is a local artist. Looking back several years, I found a photo of her with Chugg Muehler at a gallery showing. The caption read, 'Miss Potter and her fiancé, Chugg Muehler.' Even if we don't trust Jayden, I want to talk to this woman and see what she can tell us about Chugg. The more ammunition we have before rescuing Martine, the better."

"As you wish, madam," Howard said, shutting off the car.

The tiny, dingy bungalow was not at all what she'd expected. After meeting Chugg at his palatial estate, the fact that this ex-girlfriend lived in a completely opposite style home was a shock. A rock-walled entrance led to a home tucked away behind the gallery.

Before she reached up to knock, the door swung open. The woman's appearance was also not what Gemini and Howard anticipated.

Wearing no makeup, the tall, thin woman's hair was pulled back tightly in a bun. Her face was pale but she possessed a natural beauty that connected her more to outdoorsy nature types than a grandiose fellow like Chugg Muehler.

"You must be Mrs. Reed. And you're Howard Beachmont. I've heard of you. Come in, please."

Gemini and Howard exchanged surprised glances and stepped through the doorway. They were led down a dark staircase, to a large, open space. The room had concrete floors and rock walls, like a prehistoric creation.

"And you're wondering about my place. Everything here is designed to be eco-friendly. I use solar power, located on the hill behind my home for everything and we're far enough underground that it's always a pleasant temperature. I have a huge pantry and can live a year without ever opening my front door. Bryanna Potter, by the way."

She extended her hand to Gemini and then to Howard.

"I have so many questions," Howard began. "The first one being, how do you know me?"

"I approached the hospital when you were the administrator. I wanted to help them convert to solar power and reduce costs not only for the hospital, but for the patients as well."

Howard rubbed the back of his neck uncomfortably. "I'm sorry if I didn't give you a fair shake, Miss–"

"You can just call me Bryanna. I don't stand on formalities." She motioned for them to follow her as Howard continued.

"Bryanna, I'm sure you had great ideas. I was beholden to the board, and they made sure I knew it. I'm not that person anymore."

They rounded the corner to a massive living room, lit so brightly Gemini squinted. A staircase curved around a wooden balcony, where wicker-covered lights illuminated a large desk.

"This is stunning. I had no idea you could live like this underground, Bryanna," Gemini commented. "You've changed my ideas about living below the surface."

"I'm glad to hear that." Bryanna sat on a white couch and pulled her legs up under her. "You asked about Chugg when you called. That got me curious. I haven't heard that name in almost a decade."

Howard tugged on his pants, freeing his knees, and

sat. "He's a strange bird, that Chugg. What do you remember about him?"

Bryanna looked up as though she was trying to find the politest way to frame her comments. "Chugg is not an easy man. The thing you have to keep in mind with all the Muehler men is how much pressure they feel to succeed. Chugg's questionable behavior can be explained by that. Mostly."

Gemini sat beside Howard. "Yes, can you start from the beginning? Where did you meet Chugg?"

"Through a mutual friend. I was looking for investors for my thermo-friendly windows and he was throwing money around like it was trash. My friend introduced us hoping we could make a business deal."

"And did you?" Howard asked.

"That was the plan. Chugg is always looking for something better. He wanted to prove that he was the best candidate to take over the company when his father died."

"Cheese and crackers! How on earth would that man run a company?" Gemini couldn't help herself.

"Right? But he didn't see that in himself. Anyway, we started dating because Chugg thought my business mind would impress his family. Unfortunately, our first family dinner was a disaster." Bryanna sighed.

"I'm sure it's not your fault, dear. They are a diffi-cult group, to be sure," Gemini comforted.

"Oh, I know it's not my fault. I was wearing dread-locks at the time and the first thing his mother did was insult my hair. She said I looked dirty. It went downhill from there." Bryanna chuckled to herself. "I should have broken things off after that evening. They all insulted me and Chugg just sat and watched."

"How long did you date?"

"Almost a year. That's when he realized he was getting nowhere with his family and dumped me. There was a succession of women, ending with...I probably shouldn't say anymore."

"You're talking about Martine? The woman he's with now?"

"So you know. Okay, that's good. Yes, I was referring to Martine. Her father is an attorney and drew up her prenuptial agreement with Tag Junior. Ironclad. That's why she never agreed to divorce him."

Gemini raised her brow. "Until this year. She receives her last payment this month."

"Once she and Tag Junior are married for fifteen years, she'll be able to claim half of his shares in the company. If I'm not mistaken, that will happen soon."

"We knew about the money but not about shares in the Muehler Corporation. That changes things." The wheels in Gemini's head were turning. "Why wouldn't Tag just divorce her? It doesn't make sense."

"He probably wants to make sure she'll stay away from their son. If she gets what she wants, she'll never be a problem."

This went directly against Gemini's picture of Martine. She was certain Martine was the victim here, not the instigator.

Howard patted the couch, trying to get Gemini's

attention. When that didn't work, he came out and asked, "Gemini, didn't you think Chugg was overly protective of Martine? And how does her son figure into all of this?"

Gemini turned to face Howard. "Do you suppose Diego Betz knew about the inheritance? Could that be why he died?"

Bryanna stood and clasped her hands behind her head. "Diego Betz is dead? I wondered if that might happen."

Both her guests stared, mouths agape.

"After Chugg and I broke up, I dated Diego. He was such a sweet man. He came from a family just as messed up as the Muehlers."

"In what way?" Gemini asked.

"The Betz's also expected their family to succeed. If anyone didn't, they were out. Like completely dead to every single one of them." She turned the upper half of her body, keeping her feet planted in place. "Diego was the most generous of all of them, willing to sacrifice everything for a cause. When we were dating, he wanted to save the Tibetan tiger monkey. It was his obsession, you might say. Diego planned a fundraiser, and nobody came. It was the night of the Super Bowl." She shrugged. "He was never one for sports. Anyway, he hired a private investigator to go through the entire guest list, finding something from each guest's past that would embarrass them if made public. He blackmailed them into supporting his charity."

"How odd," Gemini remarked. "The man has two very opposite sides to his personality."

"If I were a gambling woman, I would bet all of that information was still in his home when he died, at least until the day after."

"Diego Betz may have been murdered for the secrets he kept," Howard announced.

"You know, I've probably told you too much. The Muehler family is so powerful, they've got ears listening everywhere. I don't want it getting out that I spilled all of their secrets."

"Thank you, Bryanna. You've given us lots of good information. We're both very discreet, I promise."

As they stood to leave, Howard pulled a card from his wallet and handed it to her. "There is a new guard at the hospital. They have a different take on things, and from what I've heard, would be interested in hearing your proposals. Feel free to use my name."

"Oh, I don't know what to say, Mr. Beachmont!"

She grabbed Howard and hugged him. He stood stiff as Gemini watched helplessly.

"It's not a sure thing, so maybe you shouldn't be thanking me yet."

"But you're giving me a foot in the door. That's more than I've had since my relationship with Chugg. He took all of his contacts with him and none of his friends have spoken to me since."

"Bryanna, I have one more question," Gemini said. "I hope you'll take this in the manner it's meant."

"Of course. Go for it, Mrs. Reed."

"Do you think Chugg Muehler is capable of murder? It wouldn't be hard to believe Diego collected information on Chugg."

She paused and sucked in air, holding it in her lungs until she couldn't anymore.

"The Chugg you see in public is ruthless. His relationships are purely for his gain, financial or otherwise. Could he murder someone? It doesn't seem to fit his character. He would pay someone else to do it, maybe, but never by himself."

"I have a final question myself," Howard added. "It bothers me that Chugg is trying to benefit from Martine at the expense of his nephew's marriage. Does he have the heart to feel bad about coming between a man and his wife?"

Gemini knew why Howard was asking this question. He and his wife ended their marriage because his wife ran off with a doctor at the hospital. It was still raw for Howard, even two decades later.

"That isn't in the realm of possibilities for the Muehler family. You look out for yourself, because in the end, that's where you get self-worth. Being a loving uncle gets Chugg nowhere. I doubt he ever even considered that."

After Gemini and Howard were back in his vehicle, Gemini rolled down the window to smell the sweet coastal air.

"Something you want to say?" Howard asked, putting the car in reverse. "I've known you long enough now that I can tell when you've got something stuck in your gullet. Spill it now, Gemini Reed, or we'll be camped out here until dawn."

"What we suspected all along is true. Rigg Muehler is innocent. Chugg Muehler is involved in Diego's death, most likely because Diego had information that would persuade Martine to leave him. And Martine, well, the poor woman needs some medical attention. I wish we had a way into Diego's place to see what we could find."

"I doubt there's anything left to see. As quickly as the murder was hushed, they cleaned that place from top to bottom. You can be certain of two things. If the killer tried framing a teen boy for the murder, he's ruthless."

"What's the other?"

"Tug overcame tremendous obstacles with his family and their misguided goals. He's a wonderful young man and I intend to make sure he knows that."

Chapter Thirty-Five

GEMINI

"You've got this, right, Olive?"

Olive scratched her head, almost pulling off the poofy grey wig she'd insisted was necessary.

"You know, Gemini, this isn't my first rodeo. I've done these undercover operations for you on numerous occasions."

"Twice, Olive. You've done them twice. But yes, I agree, you know what you're doing. Just keep Chugg occupied while Tug and I sneak in the kitchen door and up to Martine's room. We won't be long. The maid said her room is at the top of the stairs."

Olive straightened her suit jacket, the one she'd gotten from the costume closet of her retirement home.

"And you'll push the alarm button on your necklace if you really are in trouble?" Tug added.

"Will do. You gonna get that eye checked out too?"

"Feather already made an appointment for next week."

One thing Gemini Reed excelled in was striking up a rapport with anyone on any given day. After the maid gave Martine the first message, she felt comfortable trusting her again. She and Howard sat outside the Muehler mansion the previous evening, waiting until the maid left at the end of the day. Gemini gave her another note for Martine and explained she was coming back to get her.

"Oh, no, you can't do that!" the maid whispered, as if her employer would hear the conversation from around the corner.

"I'm afraid we must. The poor woman is trapped and we're her only hope. If it were one of your relatives, wouldn't you be willing to do whatever it took to free them?"

The maid frowned. "You're putting me in a no-win situation. You really have no idea what's going on here."

"I'm sure it's much worse than I imagine, dear. But we are removing Martine tomorrow. If need be, I can tell Chugg you're in on it."

She didn't feel right threatening this poor woman, whose only crime was being employed. But it was late, and she was tired. There wasn't another option.

"The maid says you can ask for Chugg and tell him you are representing Dogs in Blue charity. It is his favorite organization, and he donates regularly."

"Shouldn't you have found me a dog? To play the part?"

Gemini shook her head. "I can't explain it, but the charity is to provide shoes for the needy in Finland. They only use dogs as a fundraiser. They dress them in blue outfits and have them parade down a carpet, like a fashion show."

Olive put her hand on her forehead and chuckled. "Those rich folks have never made sense to me."

"Okay. I got the information from their last big event," Tug said, reading from his phone. "They made two million dollars by giving people the chance to sponsor a dog on their runway. You're going to go up to the door and say you'd like them to sponsor a dog, Porky, for their next runway event." He handed her a folder with a picture of a black-and-white bulldog.

"And what if he doesn't believe me? Folks don't just show up at your door anymore, unless they're trying to sell you something you don't need."

"The maid said you want to mention that the big boss sent you. That's all she would tell me, but evidently it's a big corporation with local connections."

"Okay. I'm not sure about this, but I'll do it."

"As always, I'll be listening. Tug and I are giving you five minutes to get in the door, then we're going in the back way."

Olive walked up to the door and rang the bell as Tug and Gemini found the kitchen door. Luckily, the maid had given Gemini a map of the grounds.

"Yes, Mr. Chugg. I'm here to talk to you about

sponsoring a pup. Not just any pup, but Mr. Beans, here." She produced the picture and handed it to him. "Cute little bugger, ain't he? He's gonna wear a swimsuit at the next runway event for Dogs in Blue. The big boss sent me, said you'd agreed, I just needed to pick up a check."

"How strange. I was just at Ko Industries yesterday dropping off paperwork. No one mentioned they were sending a courier."

"Oh, I'm not a courier. I'm here to convince you to spend money on things you don't want."

Gemini cringed. "No, Olive."

"Jayden Ko is connected to Chugg?" Tug whispered as they walked up to the back door.

He jiggled the knob, just as they were told to do, and opened the door.

The lights were off, so he turned his phone light on and motioned for Gemini to follow him. When they reached the stairs, Tug's body hit something. He jumped back in surprise, bumping into Gemini and knocking her to the ground.

As Tug turned around to help her up, the lights turned on. They could see they weren't alone, that three big men were there with guns drawn.

"Son, I must've been confused. This isn't our house!" Gemini exclaimed, as Tug helped her to her feet.

"Nice try, Mrs. Reed. We know who you are and why you're here. We'll be happy to escort you, and your friend in the living room, off the property," the largest of the men said.

Her face red with embarrassment, Gemini stared at her feet. She hoped Tug had a brilliant idea to rescue Martine.

"You know I'm a Muehler too. This is my uncle's house. He'd probably want me to–"

"Make an appointment. That's what your uncle wants. Let's go." The men ushered them back outside and stayed a step behind them until they reached their car. As soon as the door was open, Olive appeared.

She shook her head and talked to herself in gruff tones until she reached them.

"I'm sorry, guys. I really messed this one up. Chugg said he knew I was lying. He waited for his manservant to come and shove me out the door. Not a word about Martine."

Gemini got in the car and brushed herself off, double checking that she hadn't torn anything in her fall.

"Not to worry, Olive. It wasn't you at all. It was me. I trusted the wrong person and she betrayed us. We'll find another way to get Martine."

"Gem, are you okay? You're recovering from surgery. I feel awful for knocking you down like that."

Tug turned on the light in the car so he could assess her well-being. The minute he did that, there was a wrap on the top of the car. All three of them looked out the window to see one of the goons pointing toward the exit.

"I'm fine, thanks."

Tug smiled and they all waved as he put the car in gear and sped off.

"What a waste of time," Olive said, exasperated.

"Not entirely." Gemini cracked her window, so she could smell the coastal night air. "We found out that Chugg has a connection to Feather's Jayden Ko. I'm wondering if the two of them are working together."

Chapter Thirty-Six

FEATHER

Sorry to miss our lunch. My neighbor, Mr. Beasley fell off his porch while he was staring at Howard's new car. I'm in the emergency room. So far, looks like he'll be fine. Just a few bruises.

Feather looked at the message and then at Jayden. "So, you're taking over, even though he isn't dead. Is this like the real presidency, where someone has to be in charge at all times?"

Jayden was wearing a powder blue catsuit today. She had on a wig of striped grey and black. "It is in a way. This organization is hanging on by a thread. If someone doesn't step in and fix things, we'll lose our charter. This is my opportunity to do that."

"Why does that involve me?"

"You're the most capable person in the group. They're all well-meaning, but we can't have any more lawsuits or fiascos."

"I don't have spare time. I believe that's been established," Feather snapped. "Whatever game this is, needs to stop. I'm working with Rigg, I don't know who your ghost is and that's all I've got."

The hairs on her arms rose. "Not now!!" she yelled, startling Jayden.

"What did I say?"

"It wasn't you. I have a spirit bugging me."

"Listen to them," Jayden urged.

Feather closed her eyes.

It's time to reveal myself. My death came at the hands of another. In a car..."

"What are they saying?" Jayden asked.

Feather opened her eyes and glared.

"You interrupted and now they're gone," she replied, irritated. "My friends think you're up to no good. I wouldn't have said anything, but since you probably already know that, I'm giving you fair warning. They watch out for me."

"I'm well aware. Your boyfriend was ready to strangle me when they came for a visit. What I want for you, Feather, is to really think about all of this. Put the pieces together for yourself. Then you won't have to see me again if you don't want to. I'm telling you sincerely, you are the key to all of this. You know."

There wasn't anything left to say, for either of them. Feather Jones turned abruptly and left the hidden space behind the *Fold 'Em and Go.*

As she walked to her car, she realized that deep down, she knew. Jayden was right. It was time to put everything together.

* * *

"Tug, a few days ago I said I wanted to look into Julianne's death. Now I understand that we need to do it together. Do you mind?"

She motioned for him to join her on the couch, then she opened her laptop.

"Feath, do we really need to do this now? You are my soulmate. She was a part of my childhood."

"I know that, babe," she replied softly. "And you are mine. That's why we're doing this together. You have to trust me."

"When I was finally released from the hospital, my father sent me on a safari in Africa. I guess his idea was that shooting endangered animals would snap me right out of it." Tug rolled his eyes. "I didn't shoot anything, even though he paid for me to do so. When I came back, we pretended like she never existed."

Feather typed while he spoke, and a newspaper article popped up, showing a mangled car sitting in the midst of smashed washing machines and broken glass. There was something else.

"Tug, your Julianne ran into the *Fold 'Em and Go*. That's how she died."

Tug looked at the screen. "This is shocking. I can't believe my parents never mentioned that. My therapist encouraged me to treat her as a part of my past and that's just what I did."

Feather read the entire article, which stated Julianne had been at a party where she drank an entire bottle of whiskey. She left the party with a friend, who wanted to drive. It was never confirmed why Julianne ended up driving, but she crashed into the laundromat. The passenger the guests saw her leave with was not found in the wreckage.

"She's the ghost. She's the one who has been bothering everyone and she's been telling me what to do all of this time." It felt wrong to think of her as a nuisance. She'd been of great help. Her only reason for remaining was to help Tug meet Feather, and now to have Feather solve her murder.

"Who was with her that night?" Tug asked. "It says there were two people in the car."

Feather read the entire article again and looked up at Tug expectantly.

"Oh, no. I'm not contacting my family to ask about this."

"I have another idea."

Chapter Thirty-Seven

GEMINI

"You caught me off guard when you said your ex-girlfriend is the ghost in the laundromat. For the life of me, I never expected that."

Moments earlier, Gemini spit her lavender-infused tea all over Tug's shirt. "I'm so sorry. That struck me funny. I'm new to this monied life. I guess I'll have to learn how to act."

"No, please don't. You're perfect the way you are."

She smiled warmly. The family of choice she'd built since their move to Charming was as dear to her as the ones related by blood.

"Feather thinks there is a connection to Diego Betz's murder. She thinks that's why Jayden is pressing her to keep going."

"That would certainly be a tangled web. I'm fairly confident that Chugg Muehler is our murderer. His motive is Martine's upcoming payout. Maybe Diego wanted some. It's just devious enough of him to blame it on poor Rigg. I guess we can be thankful for your family's money and the coverup, otherwise, your nephew would be in jail for a crime he most certainly didn't commit."

Tug nodded solemnly. "I told you guys, my family is a mess."

"And now we've got to do our part. Jayden told us that my former nurse, Skye Baker, used to work for her. I'd like you to see what you can find out about her."

"I'd be delighted."

Gemini paced behind him as he worked. "My son-in-law would have researched her well enough to know if she'd been caught doing something illegal."

"He might have just looked at her credentials and not taken the time to do a background check. I would have done more research than that. You're too precious to all of us."

Gemini tapped his shoulders. "Thank you, Tug. You are to me as well." She continued with her pacing, muttering to herself about Skye's odd ways. "She could be some kind of secret agent for the government. Maybe she was sent by the hospital to torture me because of the lawsuit I won against them. Or maybe–"

"Gem, come here and look. I found something."

Gemini rushed to Tug's side, where he found a page with Skye's picture featured under a heading that read, "Muehler Holdings Stockholders celebrate huge gains with party," she read out loud. "That's not surprising."

"I don't think you're looking at the right picture. Look at the next one closely."

Gemini stared at the computer screen. "What am I looking at? It's an article about Muehler Holdings."

Tug pointed to the screen. "Right here, Martine Muehler and Principal Wellstone, having drinks at the stockholder's meeting."

Chapter Thirty-Eight

FEATHER

"Tug, it's time I told you everything." Feather poured herself a cup of tea and sat opposite her one true love.

He slathered his power oats in peanut butter and looked at her with surprise. "There's more? You told me about tutoring my brother and about the ghost in the laundromat. What else could there be?"

She removed a folded piece of paper from the pocket of her jeans. "Julianne was being blackmailed. You were the one person she trusted, but she didn't know how to get to you in the hospital where you were being treated. Your family made it almost impossible."

"Don't I know it." Tug shook his head. "That place was like prison, not because the staff made it that way, but my family refused my request for phone privileges and any outgoing mail was checked."

"That's right. She tried contacting you with no luck. She wrote you a note, explaining the danger she was in. Her plan was to let you know to look in her old hiding place. She thought that when you got out of the hospital, you would retrieve it and save her."

Tug's face fell. "I can't believe what you're saying, Feath. We were nothing by then. She had boyfriends, and loads of friends, and–"

"And no one she trusted implicitly. Except you."

"Are you telling me that I could have saved her? I'll never be able to live with myself if you say it's true." Tears formed in his eyes.

"No, my sweet, sweet, Tug. There was no way you could have saved her. You were trying to save yourself. She knows that now. That's why she's been insistent on working with me. She wants us to have a good life together."

Feather moved to his lap and wiped his tears. She kissed the top of his head. "You can read it or throw it away. It won't change anything that happened. Whatever you decide, she's at peace now and wants the same for you."

"One more time, and that's it, Rigg. I promise."

Today, Tag Junior leaned in his son's doorway with his arms folded across his chest. "It's okay, son. She wants to help you," he encouraged.

Rigg sighed. "Okay, but this is the last time. It's embarrassing."

Feather sat cross-legged on the floor opposite Rigg. She breathed deeply, nodding for him to do the same. When she felt he was sufficiently calm, she began.

"Close your eyes and think back to the day Mr. Betz died. You were in the cafeteria..."

"They were making fun of me. *'You're a freak, Muehler. He doesn't have a mommy, that's why he acts like a baby.'*"

Tag Junior winced. "That hurts me for you, son."

"Then you were told to go to the teacher's lounge," Feather continued. "Did you recognize the voice?"

Rigg shook his head. "Just the –"

"What is it, son?" Tag Junior asked.

"It wasn't my principal's voice. It was another woman. Someone I didn't recognize. That's why I hesitated."

Feather nodded.

"Good. So you went to the teacher's lounge. What happened when you got there?"

"I heard loud voices."

"This is important. I want you to think hard. What did those voices say?"

Rigg was quiet for several minutes and Feather sat patiently. She knew it was hard to trust them the first time you recognized them.

"They said...they said...don't go in there, Rigg. She's setting you up."

Tag Junior gasped and put his hand over his mouth.

"Who set you up? Was it someone you knew?"

He shook his head. "No, not someone I knew, but someone who knew me."

Tag Junior, unable to contain himself any longer, rushed to his son and put his hands on his knees. "Tell us, son. Who would want to hurt you?"

Rigg opened his eyes and looked around the room. He stared first at Feather and then at his father.

"No. I don't want to say it."

"Rigg, whoever this person is will continue to hurt others unless you tell us." Feather said calmly. "Just give us one name. That's all."

Rigg swallowed hard. "Her name is Martine."

Chapter Forty

GEMINI

"Do you want your muscle out front and visible, or in the back, waiting for a surprise attack?" Tug asked Gemini.

"Right here beside me, thank you." Gemini straightened her lemon-yellow top. It wasn't like her to be afraid, but when Skye agreed to meet her, she was still remembering her captivity. She couldn't continue to give this woman power over her. At least they were somewhere public, where Skye shouldn't be able to harm her. With Tug, Howard, and Olive all there as back up, they were an unbeatable team.

The bell over the door of *Feather Works Salon* jingled.

She heard the familiar clacking of heels and felt her stomach drop. "Be strong, Gemini," she said under her breath.

Skye stood awkwardly at the front desk. "Mrs. Reed? I'm here."

The supergroup stepped out from the Friendship Room together.

"Thank you for meeting us today. We have questions about your activities. Won't you join us?"

Skye looked from one person to the next, her stoic face unable to express fear. "I've only got a few minutes."

"That's long enough," Howard quipped.

They all sat down at the table and Gemini opened a container of her gooiest, most calorie-laden caramel bars and shoved them in front of Skye. "I won't be able to trust you unless you eat."

"I don't eat that kind of garbage. You know that, Mrs. Reed."

Olive took a bar for herself. "We could get you into a lot of trouble, Ms. Baker. You've been lying to us. S'pose having a few extra calories wouldn't kill you."

Skye took a bar and placed it in front of her, folding her hands beside it.

"Okay, I'm here, I'm taking your death bar. In your threatening text, you said you knew about my past. What is it you think you know?"

"We know you moved here to work for Ko Industries and that you betrayed them and were fired. What we don't know is what the Muehlers offered you in exchange for your information."

Skye took a tiny bite of the caramel bar. "I had a friend who lived here years ago. We went to boarding school together and then she moved back home. I wanted to see what her life was like."

"You're talking about Julianne?" Gemini gasped. "Julianne from the laundromat?"

"We were good friends, that's all. When Ko Industries offered me a job, I took it so I could see where she lived. We were so close."

Tug cocked his head to the side but said nothing.

"That day you came to track Martine down, she saw you and said, 'She can't see me with you.' Why?"

"Martine is a dangerous woman. I don't know." She put a large bite in her mouth and chewed very slowly.

"You'll have to do better. There are enough of us here, and you won't leave on your feet," Howard threatened. "I have enough resources in this community that you would disappear without a trace."

"I always check Martine's computer. The night before she was to meet you, I discovered her search history included a news article on your settlement from the hospital. We were concerned she would try to coerce you into giving her your money. That's her skill."

Gemini giggled. "You think Martine is the villain? That's rich. Skye, you tormented me for two weeks. I know what you're capable of."

Skye glanced toward the door. Howard, noticing where her eyes went, stepped in front of it and folded his arms.

"I suppose you're owed the truth." Skye leaned against the chair, draping her arm behind it. "I have done some terrible things, beginning with my school friend, Julianne. I knew about the hazing incident, where she locked a girl outside and that girl froze to death. I held that over her head every day. She did my homework, gave me cash, whatever I wanted. When she convinced her father to send her home, she thought she was through with me. I had to come up with another way to control her."

"Poor girl. You made her life miserable," Gemini commented.

"Yes, I did. I kept writing her letters, but she never responded. The summer after her freshman year in college, I convinced my parents to buy me a plane ticket to see her. She was shocked to see me, to say the least. I picked up right where I left off, coercing her into doing anything I asked. I was planning to stay, maybe go to college on her dime."

"You are a snake, ma'am," Olive remarked. "Not calling you names, just telling things like they are."

"That night, we went to a party, and I purposely handed her drink after drink," Skye continued. "I'd seen how much she was loved, how many friends she had, and it made me angry. I planned it out, I was going to get her drunk and she'd run off the road, killing us both. On the way home, she told me she was tired of living under my threats. Julianne was going to the police the next day. Even though she was drunk, I knew she was telling the truth. That's when I panicked and grabbed the wheel."

"You caused the car to crash into the laundromat!" Tug's voice shook with emotion. "You killed her!"

Skye put her hand up. "Not on purpose! I panicked. When we crashed, I was barely scratched so I got out of the car and ran. I didn't even pick up my things, I just left. I took a series of buses and ended up back in my hometown. I never got over my guilt, though." She cleared her throat and looked to Gemini for support.

Gemini turned her head away.

"That was part of the reason why I took the job, I wanted to contact her family and tell them everything."

"That's not going to happen," Tug snapped. "Not over my dead body."

"I still don't understand. How is this connected to Martine?" Gemini asked.

"I wandered from job to job, unable to keep focused on anything for too long. When Jayden Ko called me out of the blue and offered me a job, I couldn't believe it. It was more money than I'd ever seen in my life, and it was in Julianne's hometown. My first week here, I attended a party thrown by Ko Industries. Chugg Muehler overheard me telling someone I knew Julianne and he came over and introduced himself. He was Julianne's confidant."

"They used to talk all the time when we were dating. I didn't realize it continued afterward," Tug said. "Chugg always had a way with women."

"Julianne told him about my blackmail. That's when he turned the tables on me. He said he'd report me to the authorities if I didn't agree to help him. I gave him files from new projects we were working on at

Ko Industries. You won't believe this, but it made me sick. I hated doing that to Jayden, after she'd given me such a gift."

"Sounds like your whole life is about blackmail, Skye. If you're planning something like that here, you'll be in for a world of hurt," Howard said sternly.

"No, those days are done. At least I thought they were, until Diego Betz died. Chugg called me and demanded I come work for him. I told him I had another client." She nodded toward Gemini. "He insisted I come as soon as possible. He wanted Martine sedated. She's been acting erratically for years now. He's worried she'll do something..."

"Before she collects her share of the Muehler fortune. Cheese and crackers!" Gemini cried. "It's a big circle of deceit!"

"Well, aren't you the smart one?"

The entire group was startled by the presence of Martine.

"I'm not going to waste anyone's time. It sounds like you have all of the answers you need. I'm just letting you know, I've got enough explosives here to kill us all."

Chapter Forty-One

GEMINI

"Martine, I can't imagine there's anything you would gain by killing us," Skye said quietly. "None of us want your money."

Martine flipped her hair behind her shoulder. "Well, Mrs. Reed doesn't need my money, but the rest of you might. You're all in on it with Chugg. I've heard you talking to him."

"You've heard my voice all right. I was trying to rescue you, but Chugg wouldn't let me in," Olive said firmly.

"I've taken care of him. All of this time I had all of you fooled. I pretended to be confused and weak. It was the opposite. I never took one of your pills, Skye. I knew what you were up to the day you came. Having an affair with my Chugg!"

Skye's cheeks were blotchy red. "I can assure you, I'd never—"

Martine hit her with the butt of her gun, causing everyone else to gasp as she fell to the floor.

Martine stood over her nurse for a moment before gazing up at the shocked faces. "I suppose I should have let her suffer with the rest of you, but that felt really good."

"Martine, you have to know I've been shut off from my family for years. There's no way I would plot against you," Tug insisted.

"You and that weird girlfriend of yours are in need of cash. Don't tell me you didn't hatch a plan to get everything I had from me. You and Chugg worked it all out. I heard late night whisperings."

"It wasn't me," Tug replied in vain. There was no use, Martine was too far gone.

"Let me tell you a little story, Tug." Martine approached Tug and yanked on his arm until he gave in and sat down. She ran her fingers through his hair and his jaw tightened.

"I got pregnant as quickly as possible. Tag Junior wanted a child, so he was much easier than my last attempt. That boy refused. After the prenup was drawn up and my future secured, I made the mistake of telling my cousin, Diego. He thought we would work together to save the bees, or some other nonsense." She laughed callously. "I've been waiting for this day for so long. I planned Chugg's death and my exit. But then Diego got that teaching job. When he called to tell me, I knew there could only be one reason. He wanted to be close enough to take advantage of me when the time came. To save the dinosaurs, or some such thing."

"You killed Diego? Why was your son blamed?" Gemini asked.

"He was supposed to come in as the act happened. I was going to say, 'I'm your mommy, Rigg.' While he was in shock, I was going to place the knife in his hand. He never showed."

"Back up," Olive insisted. "You have to have a key card to get into the school. The principal told me she hadn't given out any new ones that week."

"Tug and I found an article about shareholders in Muehler Holdings. Martine and Principal Wellstone were there together, celebrating. I'm guessing she lied to you, Olive," Gemini said without emotion.

"My good friend, Principal Wellstone, was promised a hefty reward once I received the rest of the money I was owed." Martine smiled, her tiny teeth resembling those of a rat. "She gave me a key card under the name Chugg called me—Squeaky. Then, she had a teacher call Rigg to the lounge the day of Diego's death. We argued while he tried convincing me he had no desire for my money. I picked up a knife from the sink and tried stabbing him several times, but he was too quick for me."

"I did see your stab marks on the counter, Mrs. Muehler. You really got carried away," Olive said. "More energy than I'd have."

"My plan to have Rigg witness his death wasn't working, and I was tired of playing games, so I shot him." She smiled slyly. "I stuck the knife in Diego's chest after he died. I couldn't let him win."

"Nobody won, Martine," Tug said quietly. "Your poor son."

She seemed surprised by his comment. "When he didn't show, I was really upset. He ruined everything!"

It was ludicrous, Martine's thinking Rigg was the villain here. "Your son has people watching out for him. Special people," Gemini remarked.

"I even made an anonymous call to the police that he was the last person seen with Diego," she continued, oblivious to Gemini's words. "I should have known, the Muehlers take care of their own." She sniffed.

"Who took care of funeral arrangements?"

"My little Chuggy Wuggy. At this point, I had him convinced I was crazy, so he was willing to do whatever I said in order to keep me out of jail."

"To think we tried helping you. I can't believe I was so easily conned." Gemini crossed her arms over her chest. "You need help, Martine."

Martine looked shocked by the suggestion. "That's an awful thing to say! But it was a gift that you said it now that you're all about to die; I won't feel so bad."

"Does that include Uncle Chugg? He's loved you all of these years, Martine."

"Love?" Martine huffed. "What do you know about love? No one in this family has any idea what that is. Chugg is going to meet his fate in..." She looked at her diamond-encrusted watch. "One hour. I'm so proud of myself for this one. Skye, do you remember last night when you took me for a walk?" She looked down at Skye's motionless body expectantly.

"You knocked her out," Olive pointed out. "She won't be talking much."

"Oh well. Last night she had me out, like a dog on a leash. I told her I wanted to sit in my car alone for a few minutes. I gave her this sob story about missing my driving time, yada yada. That's when I got into Chugg's convertible. Skye didn't know it was his car, I guess. I put an explosive device on the starter."

"How did you know how to do that? Where did you get it?" Tug asked, incredulous.

"People will do anything if you pay them enough. We've got staff who are easily bribed."

Gemini tried not to panic, but the thought of them dying in the salon was too much. Feather wouldn't be able to live with that vision stuck in her head permanently. Tears brimmed in her eyes.

"Oh, Mrs. Reed. Tears have no effect on me." She stood on her tip toes and wiped Gemini's cheek.

"It's time for me to bid you adieu. As soon as the money is in my account, I've got reservations at Chez–"

Every single person in the room was shocked by what happened next––not only what, but who.

Chapter Forty-Two

FEATHER

"Thank you, Miss Jones. You saved my life." Chugg Muehler dusted himself off, after being pushed to the ground by Feather.

"My friends called as soon as they could. Martine was holding them hostage."

Chugg shook his head. "I've tried protecting her. She refused medication and as her paranoia grew, she became increasingly violent. She admitted to me that she'd murdered Diego. That's when I knew she needed to be secured until I figured out what to do with her. I couldn't bear the thought of my Squeaky in prison."

"That's no excuse, Mr. Muehler. Letting her get away with murder is not acceptable. And then the fact that she blamed her own son, well, it leads me to believe you have other motives."

Chugg blinked rapidly behind his lime green glasses frames. "Just what are you implying, young lady?"

"That Martine wasn't as paranoid as we thought. At least about this. You were after her fortune. That's why you preferred to lock her up yourself instead of notifying the authorities."

Chugg adjusted his glasses and licked his lips. "I think it's time you left, young lady. Thank you for saving me from Martine's little game, but I'm just fine now."

She shouldn't be surprised by anything any Muehler said, (other than Tug) but she found herself without a good comeback.

"Martine is going to prison. Tag Junior's lawyers are ensuring she doesn't receive her divorce settlement as we speak."

"That's all from you. Goodbye." He made a shooing motion and wiped the sweat from the back of his neck. "I suppose I'll need to call a car service. I'm not sure how one goes about getting rid of explosives."

"You won't need to worry about that." Feather smiled. "The police are on their way here also. My friends told them the entire story."

Chapter Forty-Three

FEATHER

"You've had an exciting week," Jayden understated. "I didn't see all of that ahead of time, or I would have, at the very least, informed you your life was in danger."

She cocked her head to the side and gave Jayden a lazy smile. "I'm not sure I believe that, Jayden. I think you like watching others solve the puzzle."

Feather crossed her arms and leaned back in the clear chair. "Just as comfortable as Gemini said."

"What is it you need from me now?"

"You knew that Julianne was the spirit in the laundromat, and that Rigg had our gift. You knew almost everything, and yet you let me believe you didn't. Why?"

Jayden leaned forward, placing her azure blue nails on the desk. "I was twelve when I realized I had my gifts. I was lucky enough to have a mentor who forced me to figure things out on my own."

"That sounds cruel, Jayden. You were just a kid!"

Feather was glad she hadn't been forced to come to terms with her gift at such a young age. No one in her family would have been supportive.

"I had a mentor who told me it wasn't my job to lead someone else's life. I could pass on what I learned from the spirit world and then step away. We all have a journey, and no one can take it for us."

She reached into the drawer and pulled out an item, keeping it in her tightly closed hand.

"I am supposed to be your mentor, Feather. Not just now, but whenever you need me. I'm so pleased that you discovered everything you did, without anyone dying."

"That's a definite bonus," Feather laughed. "Thanks, I will come to you with any questions from now on. It's nice to know you're here." She folded her hands over her stomach. "Tag Junior assured me he gave you double the amount he'd promised."

"And he offered you a handsome sum as well, no?"

"Yes, but I declined. I don't want to find myself in the mess the Muehlers are in. They can keep their money."

Jayden nodded. "Wise of you."

"Now that you have the funding, will you be able to regain your Gorilla status? I mean, technically I was working under the direction of the organization when I solved the ghost in the laundromat issue. By the way, she promised she was almost done here. She said she'd be leaving soon."

"Yes, I know. And yes, your accomplishments have moved us up in ranks. Since Capu had to retire, I'm taking over his position permanently. Thanks to both of our efforts, we're now officially P.I.N.C."

"Isn't that the same thing?"

"No, my dear. Pink with a C means we've jumped five ranks, to Cheetah. We're above the Portland chapter now. They've already called to congratulate us." Jayden smiled broadly. "I told them I took that with the sincerity with which it was given."

Feather giggled.

"You'll be joining us permanently, then?"

As much as she hated to admit it, having someone who completely understood her struggles with the other world was comforting.

"Probably. I'll have to think about it."

Jayden opened her hand, revealing a circular gold-colored pin emblazoned with the word, "Heroism."

"This is our highest honor. Only Capu and myself have received it before today. Your cape is on backo-rder, but I'll pin it on you in a special ceremony when it arrives. For now, feel free to attach it to your jacket."

She slid it across the table to Feather, who picked it up and admired it.

"It's lovely. What's the animal on there? Is it a lion?"

"No," Jayden shook her head. "It's a Sasquatch."

"Oh, so like a mythical creature then?"

Jayden seemed surprised. "Why do you think

they're mythical? If you join, I'll tell you that story someday over lunch."

Tug would really get a kick out of this. He might even have his own ceremony for her, complete with Sasquatch-themed paperware.

"You have my number, even if you don't join, you're welcome to call me any time. I'd...like it if we could stay in touch either way. You grow on a person, Feather Jones."

"Is that why you crafted this whole thing, Jayden? To make a friend?"

Jayden shook her head. "Not to make one, to help one. I love my life, but the one thing that makes it all worthwhile is being able to help other people. There's a reason I have this gift, and I believe it is to leave people better than I found them."

Feather felt a warmth inside her that had been missing all of these months. Her chest no longer hurt; it was cozy and satisfied.

"That's lovely. But, I need what you promised. My first day, you said you would help me solve the problems with my dreams."

"You've done most of the work."

"I put my business up for sale. I thought an employee was going to buy it, but she couldn't get funding." Feather held up two fingers. "So, the first message to take care of the portal is a work in progress. Then I figured out that the spinning was the laundromat and Julianne's story needed to be told. I can't figure out what the sheep made of steel is."

"First, let me say how proud I am of the work you've done. You've made positive lasting changes in your life. The last message involves a person, well, several people. But it's not my place to tell you."

Feather stood and pointed her finger in Jayden's face. "Now, look..."

She felt the hairs on her arms rise.

"She's got a message. Let her tell you," Jayden instructed.

You and your friends are the sheep. All quiet, each strong in their own way. The last is Stevie-the-new-girl, a sheep who rescued you all. She's got one last gift. Thank you for helping me, Feather. And for taking care of Tug.

Chapter Forty-Four

"Sorry I'm late." Feather hoisted a leg over the picnic bench and sat down beside Tug.

It was the first annual gathering of their little family of choice. Gemini supplied the blue-and-white-checkered tablecloth and all of the desserts. Olive asked the cafeteria at the retirement home to fix their potato salad. Howard made his secret recipe fried chicken and Tug brought Tug Bars. Rigg asked what he could bring, but they were all just happy to have him there.

"Whatever happened with that lawsuit?" Olive asked while dishing up a plate for Feather. "The girls at the retirement home were buzzing about it last month. Now? Crickets."

"It was dropped. Gemini's son-in-law took one look at it and laughed. He sent a letter saying his powerful firm would represent me and countersue the woman for his fees. The next day, it disappeared."

"It's good to know Brandon can be helpful," Gemini added without much sincerity.

"Where's our guest of honor?" Feather asked, looking around at the faces she loved. "I invited her too. She saved everyone important to me." She kissed Tug on the cheek and patted his hand.

"I'm right here." Stevie-the-new-girl-the-new-girl appeared with a large basket full of apples. "My family has a huge orchard. At the beginning of the season, we sell them for a nice profit. By the end, we leave them in the driveway with a sign that says, 'Take all you want,' and it's mostly a squirrel free-for-all..." She set them on the table and looked at Gemini.

"We're all so indebted to you, dear," Gemini said. "You were so brave to tackle Martine the way you did. How did you know where to find her explosives?"

"She left her phone on the reception desk and there was a tracker on it. Believe it or not, it was as simple as turning them off." Stevie-the-new-girl blushed. "Anyone would have done that."

"No, not just anyone, Stevie-the-new-girl," Tug insisted. "You also came in and knocked Martine out. That took exceptional bravery."

"I took a self-defense class last year. I was afraid to get up in front of the class and practice my skills, until my instructor said, 'You can be the sheep, as long as you're the cunning one. No one will suspect you.' That's what I thought of when I knocked her out with my blow dryer."

"A sheep made of steel, I'd say," Feather remarked, grinning.

"Have you told them?" Stevie-the-new-girl asked Gemini.

"No, dear. It's your news to share. Go ahead. We're all here now."

"As you know, Feather, I was unable to get funding to buy *Feather Works Salon*. That's when I found an alternate lender." She smiled at Gemini. "Your good friend is loaning me the money with no interest. I'd like to purchase your salon."

"My condition was that she keep the name, *Feather Works Salon*. and also allow you to work one or two days a week, whatever you want." Gemini added. "It works for all parties involved."

Feather's eyes filled with tears. "Gem, you shouldn't..."

"No tears until you've heard it all, dear." Gemini insisted. "I've been looking for a good investment. Howard drove me around and we found the perfect place."

"Are you moving? Please don't!"

"No, dear. It's a lovely warehouse at 1818 Flying High Lane. Just enough space to prepare Tug Bars with an office area for your investigation agency. I'm tired of Olive's mess in my kitchen. I'm too old to get down on my hands and knees and scrub every night." She winked at Olive and Olive gave her the thumbs up.

"You can use the money from the sale of your business to purchase baking equipment. Oh, and air conditioning. I'll insist on that."

Feather jumped up, almost tripping as she extracted herself from the table. She hugged Gemini tightly.

"We belong together, in business and friendship, Gemini Reed. Kindred Spirits, as you say."

Be the first to hear about new releases! Sign up for my newsletter here:

http://www.joannkeder.com

A Lime in Time

SNEAK PEEK

The early morning cool air caused Gemini to shiver. Even though she'd brought her peach-colored sweater and her long-sleeved windbreaker, she was chilled to the bone. It was unusual for this time of year.

"Are you excited, Gem? This is our first outing with our joint detective agency!" Feather practically bubbled over with excitement.

"Of course I am, dear. This is what we've both dreamed about for months!"

The warehouse Gemini purchased came with some leaks and unexpected plumbing problems, but now Tug Bars was officially occupying the factory floor. In the front of the building, she and Feather had a spacious office area with two desks, a break room and two big couches where they could sit with new clients.

When she retired from life as a legal secretary, she never dreamed she'd be continuing her working career as a detective. Nor had she imagined Leo would be spending his retirement recovering from a stroke.

She fanned their business cards in a half-circle on top of the purple, vinyl tablecloth and set some of her orange dream cookies on a plate off to the side. Her setup duties were complete.

Feather walked in front of the booth to inspect their banner. "Do you think it needs to be up higher?" She paced back and forth, back and forth, biting her nails.

"No, dear, it's just fine. Come over here with me and practice some of your mental calm exercises before the crowds arrive." Gemini motioned for Feather to join her in her custom-made-with-back-support chair.

Just as Feather sat down next to her friend and business partner, a voice screeched, "Isn't this the hoon-doggiest darn thing! We've got us a tent!"

The other vendors paused what they were doing to stare at the woman standing in front of their tent. A portly woman with short, pink and purple hair, she sported a bright, blue t-shirt that read, "Tug Bars, Tug-n-Olive's Creations."

"Olive, you can take it down a notch," Feather responded with irritation.

"We're glad you're enthused, dear!" Gemini added, trying to lighten the mood. "Feather's feeling nervous is all."

"Haven't your spirits told you things is gonna be fine?" Olive asked, inserting her chair between theirs.

"It doesn't work like that, Olive. They don't necessarily tell me about the future, unless it directly affects them or their loved ones."

For the past week, Feather had been visited by spirit with no face. She couldn't tell if it was a man or woman, but it was definitely in pain. When the spirit came, she smelled a strong scent of caramel corn cooking, as she did right now.

"The opening bell is in one minute!" A voice boomed over the speakers.

"Count down with me now, fifty-nine, fifty-eight, fifty-seven..."

All three women enthusiastically joined in.

"Is there a Feather Jones in your tent?"

A man's loud bark caught them all of guard.

"I'm Feather Jones."

Now that he was closer, it was obvious he was a police officer.

"Ma'am, you're going to need to come with me."

He approached her, standing so close Feather could smell the coffee on his breathe.

"What's this about? I used to work at a law firm and I know her rights. She doesn't have to–"

As Feather stood, the officer pulled out his cuffs and placed them on her wrists.

"Feather Jones, you're under arrest for murder."

About the Author

Joann Keder is an award-winning author who spent most of her formative years (over 40) living on the plains of Nebraska. When she and her husband chose to make a move to the Pacific Northwest, she came to an agreement with her soul that it was time to start writing.

Today, she creates stories about strong women and the paths they choose. When she's not writing, she and her husband enjoy nature, a good chocolate and spending time with family. Not necessarily in that order.